# The Stories

~.~.~.~

## Caroline Muntjewerf

Join the mailinglist here:
https://cmuntjewerf.com

The object next to it was smaller in size. It didn't look like a chair from what the sheet gave away. I slowly pulled the sheet and there, staring at me with dead eyes was a dog. A taxidermied dog. A German Shepherd. The fur of the poor animal was dull, one of his ears had the tip missing. His dead tongue, that dangled from its mouth, looked like it had been painted pink. The cream-coloured teeth posed a threat, ready to strike at prey any time. I was sure that this must have been the dog in the photo. Did it die of natural causes? Or at the hands of someone near, in a fit of rage? Why then, have the dog stuffed? I lowered the sheet, the dog disappeared beneath his decades-old shelter.

I gathered more courage, walked towards the life-sized painting of the dictator and stood in front of it. The aura of a being that had truly lived, made me feel uncomfortable. I stood there and looked at that face, in these eyes, when I heard a noise behind me.

I froze. A chill ran through my body. The room felt ice-cold.

From behind, a streak of light fell on the image of the man in the painting.

His face turned white as that of a corpse.

It was as if time had stopped. It became deathly quiet.

How long I stared at that stone-cold face, I do not know, but somehow I gathered the presence of mind to turn around.

Then I saw the door had swept open. I could see in the forbidden room! Without thinking I walked to the open door, entered the other room and grabbed the doorknob. Within a second I was back in the room with exhibits. A visitor gave me an indifferent glance before giving the artefacts his full attention again.

As I rushed towards the stairs I looked over my

shoulder and saw only *one* door.

The one with the sign 'Private'.

Outside, as I walked past the castle, I looked up at those windows as I had done so often. As always there was no movement behind the windows.

I reached in the side-pocket of my bag.

The envelope was still there.

~.~

# Gemma got to her feet

The girl is right. Statistically speaking a lot more people die on roads than in air crashes. Why has she been so afraid of flying all these years? More than fifty per cent of people divorce each year. Why be in denial about the state of her marriage with Harry? After twenty-five years, it is no surprise that he would want something different. And she isn't getting any prettier. Prettiness wears off once you've passed the age of thirty.

She clutches her boarding card as she lines up behind the other passengers. The young woman who checked her in, comes nearer. No, Harry has always loved *her* and no one else. He has said so. Well, in his way he had. She glimpses through the window past the security guards. The body of the aircraft looks lugubrious with the dark clouds overhead.

'Madam?' the young woman's voice sounds. She turns to face her. 'Your boarding pass, please,' she says in this convincing manner. Gemma looks down at her hands, hands that feel sweaty and are shaking. She looks for the piece of paper. It lies in front of her feet. 'I'm sorry,' Gemma whispers. She quickly bends down and reaches for the crumpled boarding card. 'You'll be fine, Madam,' the woman smiles.

She feels faint. She turns and stumbles away from the gate to let herself down on one of the chairs in the departure hall. Her hands are trembling. She lets out a gasp of breath. Get yourself together! Of course, you'll be fine! He only loves *you*. He said so.

A passenger leaves the line and walks towards her. 'Excuse me,' he says. She looks up. 'Would you mind?'

he asks. He doesn't wait for the answer and sits down next to her. 'I couldn't help but notice your anxiety,' he says. His accent is foreign. He knows what she's going through. He has been on an aeroplane once that had skidded off the runway and almost crashed. And he survived. Gemma looks at him. Not a scratch on his handsome face. But that doesn't mean he isn't hurt on the inside. 'Thank you,' she says. 'I'll be fine. Just having a touch of the cold feet.'

He gets up and offers her his hand. With a faint smile, Gemma stands up and walks back to the gate. The hostess hands her the boarding card. The man follows Gemma closely as she boards the aircraft.

'Fourteen A,' the flight attendant confirms with a friendly smile. 'Straight on, to your right.'

See? It isn't so bad. It is like boarding the bus to Swansea. Gemma slides into her seat. The man from the departure lounge takes seat fourteen C.

'Let me help you,' he says when when he sees her struggle with her seat belt. Gemma thanks him, smiling nervously.

What about that time she rang Harry in his office, and she heard someone giggle in the background? 'They're unpacking the new fabric,' had been his excuse. And that time when he was in Hong Kong. He never phoned. If she hadn't phoned him, she would not have heard from him at all. Why have they never talked about their marriage? Sure, they discuss the children, their education, the boyfriends. But what about *their* relationship?

The rain is streaming down the small window when the aircraft moves away from the terminal building. She stares out of that window and pays no attention to the safety instructions when they are demonstrated. A composed voice sounds over the intercom. Had she been mistaken about Harry's feelings for her all those years? Is her mother right? Had Frances been right?

She clutches her armrests when the plane jerks his way through the dark grey clouds. The man beside her rests his hand on her arm. 'It will be over soon,' he says. 'It's always sunny above the clouds.' His dark brown eyes are calm. They show a twinkle. A bit uneasy, she returns the smile. She looks at the grey masses that pass by the small window. They are the same colour as curtains hung around coffins in funeral homes.

Somewhere above the continent, the skies clear. Gemma has lingered over her late lunch, and now the flight attendant comes to take it away. She only has the glass of wine. It helps her relax.

'My name is Giacomo,' the man informs her. 'Why are you going to Italy?' he wants to know. He smiles in his charming way. 'I mean, with your fear of flying.' She doesn't want to answer.

'But I'm sure you have enjoyed the flight. Yes?' His wedding ring shimmers in the light of the sun. She gazes at hers. Harry always wears his, too, when he's home.

'Are you going to see your wife?' she asks him. He isn't, he'd left his wife in England. He is flying to Milan on business. She understands. Harry always leaves *her* behind.

She feels tense as she follows the Arrivals-sign inside the terminal at Milan airport. Will Harry be surprised when she shows up out of the blue? Will he be annoyed when she disturbs him? He actually never is. And besides, he *asked* her to come. She can't think why he asked her to come. He never asks her to meet him in the cities where his work takes him. He knows about her fear of flying.

She feels nauseous for not trusting him, for feeling the need to check on him.

Outside, she waves down a taxi. She tells the driver the name of the hotel where Harry always stays when he is in Milan. The ride is long, and it is getting dark. She doesn't recognize much of the city. The hotel they eventually reach, she recognizes from a postcard. She pays the driver, and she looks up at the façade of the hotel. Coloured floodlights make the building look even more conjuring.

She walks to the reception desk in the spacious hall. 'I believe my husband is staying here? Harry Bowen?'

'Gemma!'

She turns. What is Fred doing here?

' Gemma ...' He looks worried and astounded at the same time. 'We hadn't expected you here now.' He looks over her shoulder. Gemma turns to see. Fred takes her by her arm and leads her away. 'Where's Harry?' she asks.

Fred's face darkens. So it *is* true! It feels as if an unknown force is gripping her stomach, squeezing it tighter and tighter. She rushes away from the hall towards the toilets. 'Gemma, I'm sorry!' She doesn't hear.

When she finally walks out of the restroom, she looks straight into Harry's face. 'Darling, are you all right?' he asks. She trembles. Then, she notices the plaster over his forehead.

'Crazy taxi drivers in this town,' he explains, 'crashed straight into a traffic light. I'm so happy to see you! A lot sooner than I expected.'

She flew, she says.

'My darling,' he replies with pride.

She *has* to know.

He leads her to a seat. 'I'm so glad you came. I have to admit, it worries me, always leaving you on your own, a beautiful woman like you. You could have any man.'

He doesn't fool *her*. She has to know.

'I'm so proud of you. *Flying* out here.' He pulls her closer and kisses her lips.

'Happy anniversary,' he whispers in her ear. 'I'm so glad you're here. Now, we can celebrate.'

~.~

# *Suicidal*

*I*t is always a slight problem to find a good spot to park the car when he visits Joaquin. Once he had parked under the row of large chestnut trees but he hadn't considered the autumn time and on his return, his car was covered in brown leaves and conkers that had left unpleasant marks on his vehicle. Near the garden gate beside the hedge usually evokes aggravation from other road users on this narrow country lane, but it is the best option. As he closes the door of his car he recalls the last time he and Joaquin were out and about in Joaquin's car. He, Bernard, drove as Joaquin, even at that early hour, had been consuming a tad too much beer than was legally allowed.

'I didn't have anything else in the house and I had to drink something with that dry croissant.'

'Didn't you have water in your tab then?' Bernard had asked.

On the way home from the races he had taken the wheel again, for Joaquin had drowned his great losses in tubs of beer. With Joaquin sleeping it off beside him he'd been wondering about his behaviour of late; Joaquin had been a far cry from his usual self.

Abruptly he'd had to jump on the brakes. In front of him had been a herd of cows that were meandering along in the middle of the road. Before he knew it the car had come to a halt with an incredible bang against a fence that was bordering a meadow. Shocked he'd sat there until he had heard Joaquin's snoring. The cows had moseyed along. The car was a write-off, so was the fence. He'd later learned that Joaquin had a down payment on the car and hadn't taken the trouble to have the car insured.

'Insurance is for losers,' was Joaquin's reasoning.

'Yes, and who's the loser now,' he had objected.

Bernard looks at the house as he strolls up the garden path. There's a peculiar quiet atmosphere. No music blaring from open windows. Instead, a curtain flutters from a first-floor window. Not even the dog comes walking around the house, wagging his tail. As he takes another look at the surroundings of his friend's house, Bernard lets his hand glide onto the doorknob. He was sure Joaquin had said he'd be home and he was sure Joaquin would have locked up if he'd gone out.

'Jock!' his voice echoes in the hall. Bernard glances about him. Peculiar. And no dog. Peculiar, that the normally open kitchen door is now shut. His eyes flash from side to side as he walks across the hall. Slowly his hand reaches for the kitchen door and with a quick movement, he pushes it open.

'Jesus! Jock! What are you doing?!' he calls out as he sees his friend wobbling on the back of a chair, his bulging eyes staring at him as he tries to utter sound from his swollen lips.

'And what's with the rope?' when he notices the noose around Joaquin's neck. 'Jock, for Christ's sake! Here, let me help you.'

Bernard laboriously climbs onto the table as Joaquin starts making wild movements towards the chair he balances on.

'What?' Bernard wonders. 'No, it's OK,' he says as he reaches to free his friend from the rope, something he has to pay for with a punch in his ribs. 'Ouch!'

With wild hand movements, Joaquin once again points to the chair below him. Undeterred Bernard loosens the rope around Joaquin's neck; the smell of stale booze wafts over him. When Joaquin is, chokingly, about to lose his balance Bernard is just quick enough to prevent him from falling flat to the floor.

'Can I get you some water?' Bernard asks.

Pushing Bernard aside, Joaquin clambers from the chair onto the floor. 'Bernard, you bastard!' he manages to utter between the throaty coughs as he tumbles down.

Flummoxed Bernard stares down at Joaquin's bloated, red face, still holding on to the rope that dangles from a pipe on the ceiling.

'I ... I couldn't get the bloody chair out of the way,' Joaquin gasps.

Bernard is lost for words.

'And could you come down from my table.' Joaquin says, his hand clutching his bruised throat. 'You look pathetic.'

While Bernard steps unto the chair and then on the floor, Joaquin stumbles out of the kitchen.

'Joaquin!' he calls after him. 'What the hell are you playing at! I'm your friend, no harm in letting me know what you're playing at!'

Joaquin turns around. 'In case you're too stupid to put one and one together, I wanted to kill myself. Why did you have to show up? What the hell are you doing here anyway?'

'Oh no, Jock. You can't be serious. Why wou ... '

'Don't be such a sissy, Bernard! I want out! I've had enough! My wives all left me. My money is gone! I'm losing my house! My dog ... ' Joaquin can't hide his emotions any longer. He shakes his head as he slides onto the floor.

'What about your dog?'

'My dog, my poor dog,' Joaquin sobs.

'What happened, Joaquin?'

'The poor animal ... '

'Jock, don't tell me ... '

'I couldn't even feed my dog anymore.' Tears stream across Joaquin's face. 'My very own dog.'

Bernard looks down at Joaquin. 'So, what happened to him?'

'Oh, the poor sod. I've had him since he was *that* small. You know, we took him from the animal home after my last wife had buggered off. He was ... my poor dog ... '

Bernard goes into Joaquin's lounge room and searches in the drinks cabinet for a glass and something to drink. He pours the remainder from a gin bottle into the only, greasy, glass, walks back to the hall and hands the glass to Joaquin. 'Here,' he says, 'will make you feel better.'

'Thanks,' Joaquin mumbles.

'You know what your problem is ... '

'Yes, I drink too much,' Joaquin replies as he empties the glass in one gulp.

'If you've lost everything because of it, wouldn't you say it would be wiser to stop?'

Joaquin wipes his face with his sleeve and with one powerful move he smashes the glass against the opposite wall. Then he holds out his hand for Bernard to help him up off the floor.

'Bernard, you're true friend,' he says. 'I'd be dangling there dead if it wasn't for you.' He grabs Bernard by his shoulders. 'A true friend.'

Bernard smiles at him. 'I'm glad I came when I did.'

Joaquin puts his arm around Bernard's shoulder. 'Do you think you could drive me over to my sister's?'

'Sure. No worries.'

'Pick up my dog. I miss the old bugger.' With his arm tightly around Bernard's shoulders they walk out the front door.

'And Bernard, would you mind awfully lending me some money … Just until I get myself back on my feet.'

'Sure. No worries.'

'A true friend,' Joaquin reiterates.

~.~

# *The love of her life*

*D*rained after an exceptionally tedious and long day at the office, she climbs the stairs up to her flat; no lifts in *her* building. There hardly had been any 'lifts' in her existence, period. It always had been one struggle after the other until … Until last year, when Mark had appeared in her life. She couldn't say it had been a surprise for she'd had, what can be called, premonitions. Premonitions that major, extremely positive changes were about to occur. And then, there he was! She knew at once that he was 'the one'. They clicked from the start. For months, everything was more perfect than she could ever have hoped until … Until that *whore* appeared on the scene. Some asylum seeker after a 'ticket into the country'. And he fell for it. At the same time ripping her heart out, crushing it to smithereens and putting it back in her chest. It would take a clever guy to paste it up again, if ever. She opens the door to her flat. Oh well, all water under the bridge now.

A blue glow lights up her living room. She refrains from switching on the light; the clear moon presents her with sufficient brightness. She kicks off her uncomfortable office shoes and walks barefoot towards her balcony door to open it wide. A warm evening breeze flows into the room. She pulls up her favourite chair and sits in the glow of the moon. She gazes up at the starry night that looks so peaceful and closes her eyes. Often when she feels depressed, she finds that a talk with the 'Man upstairs' makes her feel better.

'Oh God, if you're so full of compassion, like they say you are, why do some people have to suffer such heartache as I've had to endure this past year? Why do you allow people to hurt an other so? I know I *begged* you to send me a man to end my lonely existence, a man who would love me! Why did you allow the man you sent, to hurt me so much? Is that what you had in store for me? Is that what all my praying brought me? Was it a lesson I had to learn? What is so educational about a broken heart? I ask you!'

Tears roll across her cheeks at the memory of last year's occurrences. She wipes her eyes and notices clouds have obscured the moon and left her flat dark. 'Typical,' she utters. 'Takes my man away and now won't even allow me to enjoy the moonshine.'

She gets up from her chair to walk to the nearest light switch when her room is suddenly bathed in bright light.

It only lasts a second.

Thunder crashes almost simultaneously. She returns to the open balcony door. 'I hope my words haven't made you angry now,' she says to the pitch-black sky above.

Another lightning bolt crashes through the clouds. The brightness is so profound she instinctively holds one hand across her eyes while with the other she reaches for the balcony door. A sudden blow throws her to the floor. Bathing in this extraordinary intense light, she tries to look up. With crashing thunder above her, everything becomes dark.

When she sees the light again, she has a feeling she's floating. She stands up and gazes into her dark room. It is then she notices a person standing not far from her, he's dressed in white. 'Hello,' she says. 'Who let you in?'

The man doesn't answer but beckons her to follow him. 'Excuse me, but how did you get in here?' The man bathes in a white, shimmering glow. With a peaceful expression on his face, he again motions her to come with him. She looks around her, the balcony door is still open.

'It's all right' she hears. The man in white holds out his hand: 'Come'. He moves towards the open door. She feels a strong urge to follow him. The light becomes more intense when she approaches him. It almost blinds her.

Then she notices the woman right by the door, she's unrecognisable with that strangely distorted face and clothes half burned.

'Come' it sounds. She follows the man in white, who is quite handsome. A warm, peaceful feeling envelops her. It's a feeling she has never experienced before. Is this what what they call 'love'? Is that man in white her *true* love? Has God finally answered her prayers?

'Excuse me, where are we going?' she wonders.

The surroundings are intensely white, she has never seen things so white before. Fluorescent white. They come across more and more people, floating past and they all look so serene! Serene and smiling. She's never seen so many people so intensely satisfied!

The man in white stops beside a man who stands separate from the others. 'Wow,' she utters.

'This is him' she hears the man in white say. 'Through human failure, he went before you, but now you two are finally together.'

The man in white moves away while she stands there holding hands with this man who then takes her other hand in his as well. An overpowering feeling of love, floods her being as she looks into his lucid deep-blue eyes.

~.~

# French bread in Germany

*I*t's a drizzly day in the small town when a woman opens the door to the *Bäckerei*. The doorbell sounds above her head, and she finds she's the only customer.

'What will it be?' the baker asks when she's barely inside.

She asks for a baguette as her eyes glance at the rolls and cakes behind the glass. The baker reaches behind him and puts a bread roll in a paper bag.

'Oh, excuse me,' the woman says, 'that should be a baguette?'

'What!' is the baker's reply.

'A baguette. You know, a French type bread?'

The baker looks about him and puts a Laugenstange[1] in the paper bag.

'A baguette, Sir,' the woman says. 'Do you have any baguettes?'

The baker looks at her testily.

' Do you know what you've been baking this morning? Do you remember baking baguettes?'

'Look, Frau, this is Germany! In Germany, we eat German bread!'

She is surprised at the baker's hostile response, but she won't allow that to intimidate her.

'Look, *Herr*, if you would have any sense about the present-day situation in Europe you would pride yourself in baking bread that isn't strictly German! Now will I get a baguette from your shop or not!'

The baker squints his eyes to mere slits. 'Frau Kundin[2],

---

1 Elongated white roll
2 Mrs Customer

I don't know where you come from and no matter what the situation in Europe is nowadays but this is still Germany with German ways and German customs!' He slams the paper bag with the Laugenstange on the counter. The woman shudders but recovers quickly. 'Are you willing to sell me a baguette or not?'

'That's one Euro twenty,' the baker lets her know and holds out his hand to receive the money. 'Or would you like more than one Laugenstange?'

The woman holds her handbag firmly closed. 'A baguette, Herr Bäcker[3]!' she says in a loud voice. She stares at him intensely while their eyes battle it out.

The baker lowers his arm that is getting tired. The woman takes to her heels and walks to the door, then briefly turns. 'And for your information, *Herr*, the Nazi-Zeit is long gone. It wouldn't harm you if you'd adjust your habits to the present day!'

The doorbell emits an aggravated sound as the woman leaves the shop. She shuts the door just a little too firmly, but she walks on, hearing the crack shoot through the door window. The outraged baker runs after her and shouts: 'That will be an expensive French bread, madam! *Die Polizei* will hear about this!'

~.~

---

3 Mister Baker

# *Homeless*

*W*ith the prospect of having to go back to that ancient apartment where I looked after an old witch of a woman, I got off the tube at Baker Street and emerged onto a dreary, dark street cluttered with people rushing from work to get the next tube home. By this time, the tourists who frequent this area had found shelter in the nice restaurants around town.

I needed something hot and comforting to take back, so before returning to the job, one of the many coffee-shops around the corner was my goal.

Not long after, I found myself rushing back to the old woman's apartment, when I spotted a skinny looking young woman sitting shivering on the pavement in the drizzly rain. Compassion overcame me, and immediately I felt guilty for walking there with my lovely soya hot chocolate, that I'd planned to enjoy in a dry place. While standing in front of the young homeless person, I offered her the hot chocolate.

'I haven't touched it yet,' I explained.

She shook her head. 'No thanks.'

'Pardon? It's nice and hot. Or don't you like hot chocolate?'

She looked at me with hollow eyes, her face was pale, her bony hands gripped her skinny knees.

Then, she put her hand in her pocket, and a Barbie doll appeared.

'This is all I have,' she said. 'Do you want to buy it?'

I looked at her. I didn't have any need for a Barbie doll, and I wasn't keen on giving her any money. I shook my head. 'Sorry.'

'I need some money for the train. I want to get out of this city and go home.'

Then I remembered the information I was given a few days ago by someone in the street in case I wanted to donate to the homeless. The leaflet was still in my bag.

'There must be somewhere where you can get help, a safe place to sleep,' I said and gave her the leaflet. 'Here, go there.' Again she looked at me with those eyes that had given up hope.

'How do I get there without money,' she said.

I reached in my bag and gave her the travel-card I'd been using. 'Here, it's still valid for the rest of the evening.'

Briefly, a glimmer of hope showed in her eyes. She took the travel-card and slowly got up off the cold pavement. 'Please, take this too,' I said and handed her the hot chocolate. 'You can take the Bakerloo Line down to Piccadilly. The place is not far from the tube station.'

I watched her as she walked into the Baker Street station. For a moment, she paused by the escalator and managed a hopeful smile before going down to the trains.

~.~

# *The Bookshop*

*S*he stands behind her counter and looks out the shop window into the street. It is not busy at this hour and now and then someone walks by. Now and then someone even glances into her shop window and then walks on. To make her counter a little more attractive, she decides to open the box with the new books that she received yesterday. She ordered a new coffee table book last week and hopes it will entice customers to spend more money in her shop. She arranges the books in such a way that they have to draw the customers' attention.

She omits the price tag of € 24.99. She reasons that if people want the book, they don't ask about the price. She places two of the books in her shop window and pastes the supplied poster to the window at the entrance. 'Hollandse Molens Belicht' (Dutch Windmills In The Limelight) is written on it in large letters plus the name of the author and the photographer who provided the photos. To lure tourists. Let's hope they can read Dutch because the descriptions of those beautiful windmills are in the Dutch language.

It is never really busy in her shop she can handle everything on her own. Nowadays it is rather quiet, most people order via the internet and she has thought about starting a webshop, but to set up such a site is not cheap. And who can compete with large companies like Amazon?

She takes another look at her recent display and shifts the top book one millimetre. Her eyes wander outside. The street is empty, and she walks to the back to switch on the coffee machine. It's almost time for coffee, mid-morning.

She takes a sandwich from her bag, and while she waits for the coffee to percolate, she goes back into the store. Outside it has started to rain softly. There won't be any customers now. The coffee maker simmers the last bit of liquid into the coffee pot and she takes her mug to pour the coffee in it.

Occupied with her daily monotonous activity, she is suddenly startled by the ringing of her shop bell. She has one of those old-fashioned bells on the door that rings when the door opens. She bought it once in a thrift store years ago. Amazed and at the same time curious, she glances through the open door of the rear part into her shop and sees a man who is looking around her bookshop with an inquiring eye. She leaves her coffee for what it is and walks behind the counter. 'Good morning, Sir,' she says. 'Can I be of service?'

The man looks at her but doesn't say anything. He is neatly dressed, in one of those business suits, but without a tie. 'I just got these in,' she says, resting her hand on the stack of Hollandse Molens Belicht. 'Very nice book. And very popular.'

The man shows no interest in her latest addition. 'Good morning,' he says. 'You have a nice little shop here.'

She nods. 'Or are you looking for another book?' she tries in an attempt to sell something on this drizzly morning.

'No, I don't really like books,' the man replies. 'Or actually, I don't have time for books.'

'Well, I'm sorry to hear that,' she says. 'But this is a bookshop. For bread, you need to go across the street, to the bakery.'

The man looks at her again. 'I understand you're the owner of this property? I may not be interested in books, but I think your shop is very attractive.'

'Oh,' she says, slightly irritated. 'What do you want with my shop? It's not for sale, you know.'

The man reaches to shake her hand. 'Van Dijk,' he says. Hesitantly, she takes his hand for the light handshake.

'I work for a production company,' the man goes on. 'Film productions, and we are looking for a location for a TV series that we are working on. Your shop fits in well with one of our main characters. He runs a bookshop.'

'Oh,' she says. 'That's all well and good, for your main character. But this is my shop and I'm not in your movie. Anything else?'

The man looks at her in that investigative manner again, and it starts to bore her. He doesn't buy anything, and she smells the scent of her cup of coffee that is now getting cold.

'I believe you don't quite understand me,' he says. 'I'm sorry, I should have been clearer. I am a location scout for Coinyard Productions and, as said, your shop fits well in the story that we are going to adapt. You will be well rewarded of course, when we use your shop as a film set for a few weeks.'

'Oh,' she says, now with a degree of interest.

An expectant look appears in his eyes. 'Are you interested in working with us?' he asks. 'It will mean, that if we are shooting here you cannot sell books in your shop. You would have to close your business for a while.'

Her thoughts start to run wild. Her shop, a movie set? 'How uh … How does that work?' she asks. 'I mean, if I have to close my shop, I have no income.'

'You will be well rewarded, and for any missed income we can also make arrangements.'

Thoughts race through her mind. She has to be honest

with herself, her bookshop is not doing that well. And having to close for a period … Then she can finally go on holiday again because that has been … has been. She can't remember the last time she took a vacation. The idea of her shop as a film set…

'Uhm, but then we need a contract … '

'Of course,' he interrupts. 'Everything will be legal. Your store isn't the only location for the series. Is it convenient for you to come to Amsterdam? Let's say tomorrow? Our offices are there and then we can talk about it, and arrange the contracts.'

He takes a business card from his inside pocket. 'Here are my contact details.'

Her hand reaches for the business card, and she takes it.

'Do you have any questions?' His voice is reminiscent of that of a schoolteacher's.

'Uh, when … When are you coming? To film, I mean.'

'This summer.' He holds out a hand. 'Then I'll see you tomorrow.'

She shakes his hand with an optimistic feeling. 'Tomorrow. Eleven o'clock tomorrow morning. Is that all right?'

'Fine. Then I will no longer keep you. Good day.' He walks out of her shop with a brisk pace. The store bell rings loud and clear. She watches him walk into the high street and glances at the business card that she holds in her hand. The logo of the well-known production company smiles back at her.

## Ein Kerlchen von drei und ein Kerlchen von fünf

Ein Kerlchen von fünf steht mit seinem Gesicht gegen einen Baum, seine Händchen vor seine Augen gedrückt. Sein Brüderchen rennt, so schnell ihn seine kleinen Beinchen tragen können, davon und versteckt sich hinter einem Bierzelt, das noch da steht von gestern. Gestern gab es ein großes Fest auf dem Schloßplatz, tausende Menschen waren zusammengeballt an dieser Stelle.

Dieses Zelt nun kommt dem Kerlchen von drei gerade recht. Rasch versteckt es sich, während sein großer Bruder eifrig zählt mit seiner Nase gegen den Baum gedrückt.

„Ich komme!" ruft er und fängt ein Bisschen verzweifelt an sich umzuschauen, denn sein kleines Brüderchen ist nirgends zu sehen.

So weit kann es doch nicht gelaufen sein.

Er schaut rings um sich. Er schaut geradeaus.

Das Kerlchen von drei guckt heimlich hinter dem Zelt hervor.

Rasch duckt es sich wieder dahinter als sein Bruder sich umdreht. Der geht auf einen Baum zu, schaut dahinter, aber kein kleines Brüderchen. Wo kann es sein? Er guckt hinter ein Metallding.

Kein Brüderchen.

Das Kerlchen von drei kommt wieder heimlich hinter dem Zelt hervor.

Wo bleibt mein großer Bruder nur?

Das Kerlchen von fünf ist ein Bisschen weiter gelaufen und guckt hinter eine Bildsäule. Kein Brüderchen. Jetzt wird es beunruhigend.

Rasch taucht das Kerlchen von drei wieder hinter das Zelt.

Das Kerlchen von fünf dreht sich verzweifelt hin und her.

Das Kerlchen von drei guckt um die Ecke des Zeltes.

Jetzt wird es ungeduldig.

Da ist sein großer Bruder.

Sein großer Bruder hat ihn endlich gesehen. Mit einem erleichterten Gesicht rennt das Kerlchen von fünf auf sein kleines Brüderchen zu.

Das Kerlchen von drei ist jetzt dran seine Nase gegen den Baum zu drücken.

Eifrig fängt es an zu zählen. „Eins, zwei, drei... " ganz bis zehn.

Das Kerlchen von fünf ist schon weggerannt und was ist ein besserer Platz um sich zu verstecken als hinter dem Zelt.

Schließlich hat er sein kleines Brüderchen dort auch nicht finden können.

„Ich komme!" und das Kerlchen von drei geht auf die Suche.

Für ihn ist das jetzt ein Leichtes. Er schaut sich um, und läuft auf die Hinterseite des Zeltes zu.

Was kann jetzt noch schief gehen?

Das dachte das Kerlchen von fünf auch.

Sein kleines Brüderchen rennt schon auf ihn zu.

~.~

## *A small boy of three and a small boy of five*

*A* small five-year-old boy is standing, his face against a
tree, his little hands pressed against his eyes. His little
brother runs away, as fast as his small legs can carry him,
and hides behind the beer tent that has remained.
Yesterday, a big festival took place at the Palace Square,
thousands of people were packed here in this square. This
tent now comes in handy for the small three-year-old boy.
Swiftly he hides while his big brother diligently counts
with his nose pressed against the tree.

'I'm coming!' he calls out and starts looking around, a
bit despairingly; his little brother is nowhere to be seen.

He can't have walked that far.

He looks around. He looks ahead.

The small three-year-old boy secretly peeks from
behind the tent.

Swiftly he dives in hiding again when his big brother
turns around.

The small five-year-old boy walks towards a tree;
looks behind it, but no little brother. Where can he be? He
looks behind a metal structure. No little brother.

The small three-year-old boy furtively comes from
behind the tent once more.

'What is keeping my big brother?'

The small five-year-old boy has walked further on and
looks behind a statue. No little brother. It is starting to
become alarming now.

Swiftly the small three-year-old boy dives behind the
tent again.

The small five-year-old boy turns around
despairingly.

The small three-year-old boy peeks from behind the tent.

He's getting impatient now.

There is his big brother.

His big brother finally spots him. With a relieved expression on his face, the small five-year-old boy runs towards his little brother.

Now it is the small three-year-old boy's turn to press his nose against the tree.

Diligently he, too, starts counting. 'One, two, three...' all up to ten.

The small five-year-old boy has already run away, and what is a better place to hide than behind the tent? After all, he hadn't been able to find his little brother there either.

'I'm coming!' And the small three-year-old boy starts looking.

For him, it's as easy as pie now. He looks around and walks towards the back of the tent.

What can possibly go wrong?

That's what the small five-year-old boy also had in mind.

His little brother already rushes to meet him.

~.~

# *Santa in Broken Cross*

*T*he snow looks pretty. It made me lose track of time. It's already getting dark.

I'd better hurry home, Dad will be worried. Although, when I have Reno, my dog, with me he knows I'll be all right.

'C'mon boy, we have to hurry.'

Reno lifts my hand with his large head, he likes doing that when he wants to say: 'I'm not stupid, I know I have to get you home.'

I grab his neck-fur and let him pull me along a bit.

I got my dog when I was three years old, Dad gave him to me as a pup. This was just after my mother died. I remember little of my Mum, just that she was the sweetest person and very pretty. My Dad says I look like her, same hair, same face.

My Dad is a quiet man, not many people like him, but that's because they don't really know him. Living so far out of town doesn't help much of course. Our small farm is all the way back in the fields with a large forest to go through before reaching it.

Boy, it's really getting dark now, it must be those snow clouds making it look darker, it's not even four o'clock yet.

'C'mon Reno, we have to hurry. I don't want Dad to think we got lost.'

We're running, I can barely keep up with him. He's such a large dog and very strong, he's a Pyrenean Mountain dog. Completely white, but he has two brown freckles on his nose, very unusual my Dad told me, that's why he picked this one for me.

Boy, this snow is getting heavy to walk through.

'Look, Reno, I can see the house.'

I don't really need to tell him that, he's a clever dog. He pushes me along, he wants to get me home for he knows I have something to tell Dad.

I kick off my boots and shake the snow off my coat before going into the kitchen. Reno shakes his coat, too, before he goes into the house.

'Dad! We're back! … He must still be in the shed, Reno. Let's make some hot tea.'

Thank God, Dad lit the fire. He always knows when the weather changes.

I wonder if we will have a Christmas tree this year. I've been asking Dad for years. My father doesn't like to celebrate Christmas for it reminds him too much of Mum.

I told him: 'I'm ten years old now, Dad. I *really* want a Christmas tree this year.' He only looked at me as if he couldn't believe that I was really already ten years old.

I think this year we should get a Christmas tree for I have invited someone for Christmas.

'Hello, sweetheart. I'm glad you got back all right.'

He pats me on the head, he usually does that when he wants to say he loves me.

'Oh Dad. I had Reno with me, we were fine.'

I give him his tea. He always works so hard, never anyone to look after him. He only had two women friends since Mum died, but neither one of them liked living with us.

'Dad?'

'Yes?'

'You know my teacher, Miss Jones, don't you?'

'I thought her name was Miss Cratchet.'

'No, Dad. I don't mean that old hag. We have Miss

Jones now, she's *really* sweet.'

He sips his tea, he likes it hot.

'What about her.'

'Well, don't get mad at me, Dad, but I've invited her to spend Christmas dinner with us.'

Oh boy, Dad's face drops.

'I mean, she doesn't have anyone here, being new in town and all, and ... Oh Dad, you will love her, she's *really* nice. And I felt sorry for her.'

He puts his cup down, and he hasn't even finished his tea yet.

'You know the policies in this house when it comes to Christmas, Marie.'

Oh, I *so* don't like it when he says that.

'You're being selfish, Dad.'

'Don't get smart with me, young lady.'

Bummer. That didn't go well.

'And, what about my Christmas tree?'

'Marie ... Better start dinner.'

This is not going well at all. I put my hand on Reno's head, he always comes to my side when he knows that things aren't going well. Sometimes I wish he could talk and I could ask him if he has any ideas. If Dad could only *meet* Miss Jones. How can I get him to meet her? She really is a sweet lady, and she's not married.

Luckily, the snow has stopped falling, it's easier to walk along the forest path now. On the way to school, Miss Jones meets me and Reno. She lives out of town, too. But she's all alone, her only sister lives all the way up north. She told me this. Miss Jones looks like my mum, from the photos I have of her at least.

'Your father all right, Marie?'

'Yes, he's fine. I told him I invited you for

Christmas.'

'And? Was he pleased?'

What can I tell her, Dad hasn't even given his consent yet. I don't want her to think she's not welcome in our house.

'It always takes my father a while to get used to the idea of having visitors.'

My dog now walks between us. He knows good people when he meets them, and he has always liked Miss Jones.

'Be sure to let me know when he makes up his mind.'

'Miss Jones, believe me, it won't be a problem. You *really* shouldn't be sitting in your house alone on Christmas Day.'

She looks at me, and has a hand on my dog's head.

This is a good sign, Reno doesn't shake her off.

We walk on. School isn't far anymore once we're through the forest. The snow glistens in front of our feet now that the sun starts appearing from beyond the ranges. The day looks beautiful.

'Will we decorate the Christmas tree today, Miss Jones?'

I'm all excited about that, for it's the only time I get to help decorate a Christmas tree. At home, of course, we haven't had a tree since Mum died.

'Yes, Marie. Today we will decorate the Christmas tree with the pine-cones we've gathered in the forest and the beautiful garlands you've made.'

I look at her, my face must be gleaming. Reno also smiles at Miss Jones. Dogs do know how to smile, you know.

I'm still at school. Miss Jones has wondered why I haven't gone home yet. She's worried I won't make it before dark, but I *so* like the Christmas tree. I can't stop looking at it, I just sit here with my dog next to me looking at the twinkly lights and shining little stars we've put in there.

On the top is an angel. Miss Jones made it especially. This angel looks a *lot* better than the one Miss Cratchet always put in there, that was just a worn out old thing.

'Marie, I really think you should go home now.'

Miss Jones is still here too, she needed to do some work before going home. Reluctantly, I get up. She's right, I shouldn't be walking through the forest after dark.

'See you tomorrow, Miss Jones.'

Miss Jones looks a bit worried while my dog and I walk out of the classroom. She shouldn't worry when I have my dog with me.

The church bell chimes 'one' when we walk through the town on the way to the forest path. There's a beautiful Christmas tree in front of the church, too.

Gosh, it's 4.30!

'Reno, we have to walk fast. C'mon boy.'

He hurries me along. The skies are clear but it's dark quickly so close before Christmas.

Between the trees it looks darker than in town. I'd better not let go of my dog, although, he would never leave my side. His coat is nice and warm.

'Not too fast, Reno, the snow is slippery.'

He pushes me along … I stumble.

'Ouch!'

My ankle hurts. I have to sit down a moment.

'Reno, come on, boy.'

He stands in front of me. He barks.

'No, boy. My ankle hurts, I need to rest a little.'

He barks again.

'OK, but we have to go slow.'

I grab my dog's fur. He pulls me up.

'Slowly, boy, slowly.'

He understands, and he knows that I shouldn't be sitting in the cold snow. We won't be back before dark now. I hope Dad is not getting worried.

'My ankle, Reno, don't go too fast.'

Boy, this is tiring, limping with one foot through the thick snow. My face is hot.

'Let's rest a bit, Reno.'

My dog is impatient, he gets nervous when he hasn't brought me home before dark. I wait by his side, lifting my foot, it really hurts now. Maybe I shouldn't be standing on it. But we need to get home.

'Go on, boy, but slowly.'

He looks at me, he knows I'm hurting.

'It's OK, boy, as long as we get home.'

Slowly we move on. What time is it? It's getting really dark now. We should have been home hours ago. Where's the house? I don't see any lights through the trees. Or? No.

'Are we there soon, Reno? Can you see the house?'

Yes, there is a light! But it's moving.

'Marie!'

Who's calling? It doesn't come from that direction.

My dog barks and we stop.

'Marie!'

It's Miss Jones' voice!

'Miss Jones! We're here!' Thank God she's there.

'Marie!' My dog barks. That's Dad! That's his torch!

'Dad! We're over here!'

My dog and I wait for Dad and Miss Jones to reach us.

'Marie, sweetheart. Are you all right? Why have you

left school so late?'

'I'm sorry, Dad. But I've hurt my ankle, we couldn't go fast.'

Miss Jones looks at my Dad.

'I'm sorry, too, Mister Thompson, I shouldn't have let her stay so late. It's just, Marie was so entranced by the Christmas tree and … '

'Christmas tree, aye.'

Dad isn't pleased. 'Nothing but trouble those things bring.'

He lifts me up in his arms to walk us back to the house.

'Mister Thompson! If you would let your sweet girl have a Christmas tree, she might just rush back home to you sooner!'

*That* was Miss Jones, I've never heard her speak *so* severe.

My dog stops, Dad turns around. He never even introduced himself to Miss Jones.

'Miss Jones, I presume.'

Miss Jones looks at him with a strict face. My dog walks towards her and pushes her arm with his head. This is a good sign, he wants her to come with us.

'I was worried about Marie, too, Mister Thompson. That's why I chose to *walk* through the already dark forest to see if she had reached home all right, instead of taking the ride I was offered.'

Dad just looks at Miss Jones. Why doesn't he say anything?

'I'm sorry, Miss Jones. Better come with us first, then Dad can take you home in his truck later on.'

Dad looks at me.

'It's the least you can do, Dad.'

Dad motions Miss Jones to come with us. My dog

pushes Miss Jones forward. This is a very good sign.

I'm sitting on a chair by *our* Christmas tree, my sprained foot rests on a cushion. Close by is my Dad sitting at the kitchen table with Miss Jones. My dog stands between them. I see him lift up Dad's hand with his head and he pushes it towards Miss Jones' hand. Reno does that when he knows two people should be together. This is a very, very good sign.

I look at the twinkly lights in our Christmas tree, and the beautiful angel on top.

Miss Jones made it especially.

~.~

# *Horror*


'*G*ood morning darling!' Godfroy calls out to his wife Demelza, who is taking her breakfast with small nibble-bites. With a flamboyant swing, Godfroy lowers himself onto one of the high, wooden chairs that line the long table.

'I'm sorry I haven't slept with you last night but you know, that book *needs* to be finished.'

'Dearest, don't tell me you've worked all through the night!' Demelza cries out horrified, and with a sigh: 'You look it too, you look dreadful.'

Godfroy glances at his wife. 'You don't look that hale and hearty yourself either. You're so pale?!'

Demelza reaches for her head. 'I do feel a bit under the weather, I felt giddy when I rose this morning.'

'Is it the 'first of the month again'?' Godfroy asks. He motions the butler, Malachi, who virtuously waits for orders in a corner of the dining-hall.

'Noooo, dearest, you'd know when *that's* the case.'

Godfroy bends his head a bit and says with a twinkling in his eyes: 'You're not uhh … '

'But dearest … No, of course not. I just had such strange dreams last night.'

'Coffee and some scrambled eggs, Malachi, thanks,' Godfroy says. 'Strange dreams?'

Observedly, Godfroy looks at his wife. 'You haven't been visited by that vampire again, have you?'

'No. Well, I don't know. I can't remember a thing.'

Godfroy jolts out of his chair and walks towards his wife. He pulls the collar of her dressing gown aside. In her neck, two tooth marks are still clearly visible.

'Just as I feared!' Godfroy calls out.

Demelza feels her neck. She hadn't even noticed yet.

'Darling, I've had it. He's got to go!'

'But dearest, he's family!' Demelza says.

'Family!' Godfroy says in a loud voice. 'A great-great-great-great … great grandfather can hardly be called family! That man should just have died when it was his time. But no, mister needed to play the vampire so desperately!'

Angrily Godfroy sits down again. Malachi puts his breakfast in front of him.

'Please, Sir.'

'Thank you, Malachi.'

'I do feel … ' Demelza begins.

'Darling, *really*, this cannot go on any longer,' Godfroy interrupts her. 'You won't have any blood left!'

Demelza pulls an innocent face and says teasingly: 'Well, then I could take some of yours again.'

'Certainly not!' Godfroy cries out. 'That one time was more than enough! It took at least two weeks for those holes to heal.'

'Now you're exaggerating, dearest,' Demelza says.

'Anyhow,' Godfroy grumbles, 'he goes. If he would *work* for his living. But no, just lies sleeping in that coffin all day. Why can't he work around the garden a bit?'

'Dearest,' Demelza says soothingly, 'you know that he can't take daylight.'

'Then he can do it at night. Besides, talking about gardening. Didn't I hang garlic on our bed?'

'Oh,' Demelza says, 'I took it away, it was so smelly.'

'Fine! Enough!' Godfroy says determinedly. 'Malachi, get Madam some Echinacea herbs, for those wounds in her neck. Where's Roderick?'

'In the stables, Sir.'

'Excellent,' Godfroy says. 'I will now drive that vampire-grandfather out of the cellar.'

Demelza opens her mouth to say something.

'Not another word, darling,' Godfroy says. 'He can go and suck someone else's wife dry for a while.'

Godfroy strides out of the dining-hall and enters the broad corridor. He rushes to the far end to leave the castle at the back. A gust of wind enters the house when he opens the large oak wood door. His coattails are whipped up and almost blind him, but he rips the slip away from his face and strides across the courtyard towards the stables.

'Roderick!' He enters the stable as his equerry turns his head. 'Yes, Sir.'

'We have a problem. Do you know about that vampire that has been living in the dungeons?'

'A vampire, Sir?'

'Yes. A vampire!'

'Well, I have heard whispers. Never thought much of it, Sir.'

'Well, get prepared to think something of it, for we have to catch him and chase him away.'

'Do you think that's wise, Sir? They can be very vindictive.'

Godfroy's face shows surprise, he isn't used to be contradicted. 'Get on man! Stop whimpering! Come along!'

Godfroy rushes out of the stables, closely followed by Roderick. The wind is strong and almost pushes them back but they fight against it and as quick as they can, walk around the large castle to enter it by a hefty wooden hatch on the side. Godfroy pulls the hatch with all his might. 'Help me, man!' he calls out. Roderick now also pulls the hatch and soon a large entrance hole appears.

Steps are going down and Godfroy takes a glance inside the darkness. 'Looks like we need some torches.'

'Sir.' Roderick puts the deed into action and rushes back to the stables. He soon returns with a burning torch that Godfroy grabs from his hand. 'Let's go.'

'Sir.'

'What is it?'

'Maybe some items that would scare him away?'

'What do you mean, man?' Godfroy impatiently stops halfway the steps.

'I've heard that vampires are not partial to garlic.'

'Are you afraid to come down with me?' Godfroy asks annoyed.

'No, Sir.'

'Get on, then!'

Godfroy moves down the steps, holding the torch in front of him to light their way. Once down, they see a damp corridor. Here and there water drips from the ceiling.

'Mm,' Godfroy mumbles. He lights the area and sees a few inlets. 'Last time I was down here was with my brother when we were wee lads. We used to play Pirates down here.'

'Any sign of the vampire then, Sir?'

'God no. He would have eaten us alive. No, he's a relation of my wife. Damn ancient grandfather.' Godfroy lights the path and they move on. He points the torch towards the inlets but they prove to be empty. Slowly they move on. 'There must be a place around here where he is hiding. Be on the lookout for a coffin,' Godfroy says.

'A coffin, Sir?'

'Yes. That's where he sleeps in. When he's not bothering people at night … '

Roderick wrinkles his forehead. 'Strange creatures.'

Suddenly they feel a draft and Godfroy whisks the torch in that direction. The sudden move almost extinguishes the torchlight.

'Please, Sir. Careful.'

When the torchlight gains its flaming strength again they see some movement in a space they were just passing. Godfroy walks towards its entrance. A strange-looking bench is visible in the room. 'That was never here when we were wee lads,' Godfroy whispers. Slowly they move towards it and Roderick dares to lay his hand on it, but almost immediately pulls back when the top of the bench moves. Both men quickly take a step back. An invisible hand lifts the wooden benchtop.

'That's not a bench, it's the coffin,' Godfroy says. With eyes wide open they witness the coffin slowly opening itself entirely. It is empty. All of a sudden the lid smashes to the floor.

'What the … ' is all Godfroy can utter. Roderick's eyes show fear. 'Where's the damn … ' All of a sudden they are on the floor and it is pitch dark. A cloth is draped around them and they feel an icy coldness. 'Sir! Are you all right?'

'What the hell … ' Godfroy says.

'Sir, we have to get away from here.'

'Good observation, Roderick!' Godfroy sounds irritated and annoyed. 'But we can't see a darn thing!' He pulls the cloth, trying to get from under it. 'Help me, man!'

The men struggle to free themselves from the strange cloth that is draped around them. Finally, they succeed in standing up and they try to find their bearings. Roderick fumbles in his coat pocket and takes out a small paper box, containing matchsticks. He lights one immediately by scraping it against the hard stone wall.

'Excellent,' Godfroy praises.

As soon as there is a bit of light in the darkness they hear a scream, and again, that strange draft. Roderick notices the torch that had gone cold and quickly lights it before his matchstick goes out.

'Well done, man!'

It is now that they see an old man hunched against the wall, streaky grey hair falls over his arms that he uses to hide his face with. 'Put it out! Put it out!' his creaky voice sounds. 'I can't bear it! Put it out!'

Godfroy's face takes on a mean look. 'No, we will not put it out. You have to leave. Leave my home and hearth and go live somewhere else!'

The old man whimpers, his bony shoulders tremble. 'Please, Sir. It's so dark. Where am I to go?'

'What about, heaven? Where all good vampires go!'

'Sir … ' Roderick tries to say something.

The old man's creaky voice trembles: 'Vampire? Vampire? What are you talking about?'

'About *you*!' Godfroy calls out. 'For years you have bothered my dear wife with your sucking blood business. It's now over!'

'Sir … ' Roderick tries again.

'Me? Suck blood?' the old man says.

'Don't pretend you know nothing about it!' Godfroy calls out. 'Pack your things, and go!'

Godfroy shows no pity for the old man who still sits on the ground, shivering in his vest and pants, his bare feet covered in mud.

'Sir. Sir, I think you should know … '

'Know what!'

'This is old man Nate. He has been missing from the village for the past week.'

'What! Don't tell me rubbish, man! How does

~ 49 ~

someone from the village end up in my dungeon! Was he breaking and entering my property?' Godfroy adds with sarcasm in his voice. 'Now, that is not entirely legal!'

'It's that man,' the old man's voice sounds. 'That horrible man. He's been keeping me prisoner … ' he finishes with a whining whimper. 'Prisoner … '

Godfroy is suddenly clear-headed. 'Do you mean … there's two of you?!'

'No, no … He goes out and then he comes back. I'm his prisoner … '

Not inclined to take chances, Godfroy walks towards the old man and, somewhat roughly, inspects his neck. 'Where is he now?' Godfroy demands when he has determined there are no bite marks.

'I don't know … I don't know. Please, Sir. Take me out of here.'

'Sir. We have to take him back to the village. People have been wondering what happened to him.' Roderick takes the strange cloth, that does resemble a cloak, and puts it around the old man before helping him to his feet. 'Come with us,' he says.

'What about my vampire?' Godfroy demands. 'I want him out!' Roderick motions to the old man and without saying another word Godfroy goes ahead to light their path and before long the three of them are outside where clouds race across the sky and wind blows fiercely around the castle. It is now that Godfroy can have a good look at the strange cloak that Roderick draped around the old man. 'Is he always wearing that? Godfroy asks the man.

'Yes, he sleeps in it too.'

'He sleeps in it? Can you tell us where he sleeps?'

The old man shrugs his bony shoulders. 'Somewhere down there.'

'Well, Roderick, it looks like we have to go down

again. Take him to the kitchen and let the maids feed him something warm.'

He watches as Roderick and the curved figure of the skinny old man walk towards the servants' entrance of the castle. He then turns his gaze in the direction of the hatch they just came out of. He is still holding the burning torch and after a few seconds of deliberation, he attempts to go down again.

When Roderick returns a while later, he finds his master halfway the steps. There is hesitation in the latter's demeanour. 'I wonder, Roderick, I wonder if that old man is not the vampire-grandfather that has been living among us all these years.'

'Highly unlikely, Sir. Old man Nate is well-known, he has been living in the village for as long as I can remember.'

'Yes, of course he has. And he is hundreds of years old, Roderick. Of course everyone knows him.'

'Sir, beg your pardon, but vampires can't take daylight.'

'Meaning?'

'He would have collapsed and shrivelled to dust, Sir, as soon as we came out of the dungeon.'

Godfroy looks at his equerry with suspicion. 'You seem to know a lot about it.'

'I'm sorry, Sir.'

'You saw his fear when you lit the torch, he almost went mad! Wouldn't you say that that was an indication of fear of light?'

'Yes Sir, but when we were outside in the daylight, he was his usual self again.'

'Mm.' Godfroy mumbles. 'Come along.'

They follow the steps down and a while later find themselves in the stonewalled room where they discovered the old man. Godfroy shines the torch onto the coffin and they see it has closed itself. Roderick takes a step back as Godfroy starts pulling the top.

'Help me, man,' he says in a loud whisper. With shaking hands Roderick comes near and touches the solidly closed cover.

'Get yourself together, man,' Godfroy says. 'Don't we have a tool of some kind?'

Roderick slides a trembling hand in one of his pockets and takes out a hoof pick. Godfroy grabs it from him and hands Roderick the torch. With stabbing moves Godfroy begins to attack the lid. In vain. There is no movement.

'Do you think … he's in there, Sir?'

'Where else would he be?' Godfroy replies with annoyance. He stabs the lid a few more times. 'Damn.'

He slowly moves away from the coffin and leans against the stone wall.

'Begging your pardon, Sir, shall I get another tool?'

'You're not leaving me here by myself, Roderick! God knows what will happen.'

Quietly Roderick moves away from the coffin as well and stands next to Godfroy. The torch he's holding starts to lose its light.

'We have to push it,' Godfroy says. 'Push that lid off.'

Roderick is not certain but he puts the torch against the wall and follows his master. The flickering flame sends eerie shadows along the walls. They move closer to the coffin and with all their might they push its cover so it will open and reveal what is inside. After a few hard pushes, there is movement and slowly they succeed in shoving the lid aside. One last push brings a cold draft into the room and the lid falls to the ground with a loud thud. It makes them both jump a step back. Roderick looks on with fright as Godfroy collects himself and he casts an interested look inside the rough wooden coffin. He stares at the white face of the ancient man who lies there as if dead.

'Is he … ' Roderick whispers with a shiver in his voice.

'No, he's not. He's pretending. Look, his hair, jet black. Old dead people don't have jet black hair. It must be from all that bloodsucking from young maidens.'

'You know what needs to be done now, Sir.'

'Is that a question?'

'No Sir.'

Godfroy looks at Roderick with expectation. 'Well?'

'If you want to be rid of him once and for all, Sir, you need to … '

Godfroy casts him a questioning look. 'Need to?'

Roderick sighs. 'You need to impale his heart with a wooden stake.'

'What! But that is … that would be … that would be murder. I'm not a murderer!'

'You said that he is hundreds of years old, Sir. Might he not have died a long time ago?'

'If he had died when he should, we would not have this problem right now, Roderick! He keeps himself alive with the blood of young maidens.'

'That is not legal either, Sir. Sucking blood. So, you would do everyone a favour. You will not be sent to prison.'

Godfroy gives him a thorough look. 'You're well educated all of a sudden.' He takes a step back. 'I'm not impaling anyone! You do it.'

'Sir. I … I … ' is Roderick's horrified reaction.

'See? You don't want to do it either!'

Somewhat indecisive they stare into the coffin at the intensely white face that is encircled by that jet black hair.

The almost serene image of the vampire calms them and they take a long look at him. Immaculate white shirt, black bow tie, black pants. Black shoes that are somewhat muddy.

'Let's just chase him away,' Godfroy suggests. 'Get rid of him. Let him invade someone else's dungeon.'

Roderick shrugs his shoulders and nods. It's Godfroy who takes the first initiative. He slowly slides his hand under the shoulder of the white-faced vampire. 'Help me, man,' he hisses through his teeth. The coldness of the undead body sends shivers down his back. 'Take his feet.'

Roderick acts with caution as he takes the skinny ankles of the vampire. 'He won't wake up, will he?'

'Let's not worry about that now. Lift him.'

They slowly lift the undead figure out of the coffin and in the direction of the exit. 'Wait.' Godfroy realizes something. 'I don't know about you, but I don't have night vision. Get the torch.'

'Sir … ?'

'We won't be able to see a darn thing without that bit of light.'

'Where will we put it, Sir? We need both hands … '

Godfroy rolls his eyes. 'Good observation, man. Lower him.'

With great care, they lower the vampire to the floor. Godfroy takes the torch that by now has almost lost its ability to light their path. 'Quick, man. We will soon lose the only light. We can just make it.' He puts the handle between his teeth and carefully they proceed. With the undead man as stiff as a plank between them they make their way to the steps. Godfroy tries to climb up with his back turned to the stairs, holding the vampire in his armpits. Roderick pushes the stiff legs upwards, a movement that almost makes Godfroy lose his balance.

'Careful, man!'

The upward pushing and shoving of the stiff undead soon result in Godfroy throwing it on the grass outside the hatch. Godfroy falls onto the grass next to it and he heaves a sigh of exhaustion. Roderick clambers the last two steps and also appears in the daylight. The clouds have been chased away by the wind and now the sun brightens the surroundings.

Godfroy stands up and inspects the vampire. He has a closer look but there is no movement whatsoever. 'I thought you said they can't take daylight?'

Roderick now also has a closer look. 'That is the general conception, Sir.'

Both men are bent over the undead figure, trying to establish its condition. 'Mm,' Godfroy expresses. 'Maybe he was dead all along. He's as cold as death.' They keep their gaze fixed on the white face, waiting for a reaction. Just as Godfroy extends his hand to touch it, the undead's eyes open wide. Both men jump a couple of metres back, but they look on with inquisitive apprehension to see what the strange being might do next. With his arms, the vampire shields his black eyes against the bright sunlight and an excruciating scream escapes from his cold lips.

'He misses his cloak,' Roderick says. 'They hide in their black cloak.'

Godfroy casts him an ironic look. 'You're well informed about the subject. So, what is he going to do next?'

He needn't have asked. Before their eyes, the vampire comes to life and makes a run for it, but Roderick is quick to react and slams the hatch closed.

'*Not* in there!'

The undead man lets out a scream so loud and unbearable that it can be heard in the village. He falls to the ground, his arms covering his head, his whole being is shaking. Suddenly, his contorted body convulses. Godfroy and Roderick look on with morbid interest.

'Look at him, not so dead after all,' Godfroy observes. His curiosity drives him a bit closer to the strange writhing creature. And before his very eyes, the figure disappears into nothingness. Roderick presently moves closer to see his master shuffling his boot against the pile of dust that was the vampire-grandfather.

They look at each other with contented faces, as the wind picks up the dusty remains and blows them in every direction.

In one of the windows above them, Demelza's bitter face is visible. She has observed it all with gleaming black eyes.

~.~

## Verbotene Liebe

*N*aar het Oostfront moest hij, mijn Ernst. Het was in een tijd dat het niet mocht, je inlaten met een Duitser, en nog wel een Duitse soldaat. Later ben ik getrouwd, een 'moetje' heette dat vroeger. Ik was al vier maanden zwanger toen ik trouwde. Met een Nederlander, een aardige man en ook wel knap, maar toen onze vijf kinderen geboren waren, begon hij te drinken. En geen slappe thee, hoor. Hij had de smaak voor alcohol te pakken. Hij is er niet oud mee geworden. We waren toen al gescheiden, van tafel en bed. Nee, *echt* scheiden wilde ik niet want als je getrouwd bent, is dat in voor -en tegenspoed.

Maar hoe zou mijn leven verlopen zijn als ik de kans had gehad met Ernst verder te gaan? Hij was zo'n lieve jongen, maar in die tijd was het onmogelijk geweest. Na de oorlog kwamen de beelden van Nederlandse vrouwen die kaalgeschoren werden en belachelijk werden gemaakt omdat ze iets hadden gehad met de Duitsers.

Mijn vader was niet blij toen hij er achter kwam dat ik iets had met een Duitse soldaat. Stiekem zag ik Ernst toch, hij was lief en we waren verliefd, maar het was oorlog en toen moest hij naar het Oostfront. Hij gaf me een foto, die ene waar hij opstond met zijn hond. Gewoon een knappe jongeman met geen spoor van oorlog om hem heen. 'Von deinen lieben Ernst' staat er op de achterkant. Die foto had ik nog jarenlang op mijn nachtkastje staan. Een zwart-witte herinnering van mijn lief.

Ik zie hem nog gaan. In die tijd werkte ik als huishoudelijke hulp bij de dokter en ik stond op het balkon toen Ernst met een legervriend op weg ging naar het station aan het einde van die straat. We zwaaiden. Ik zwaaide, totdat zijn blonde haardos uit het zicht verdwenen was. Hij stuurde nog een aantal mooie brieven. Maar opeens werd het stil. 'Wann ich nog am Leben bin, komme ich wieder zu Dir, um zu heiraten,' had hij gezegd. Maar ik hoorde niets meer. Was het toch gebeurd waar ik bang voor was geweest? Was hij aan het Oostfront omgekomen?

Als de oorlog voorbij is, zien we elkaar weer. De oorlog was voorbij, en ik ontmoette Jan. Met hem ging ik verder ...

'O, bent u er al?'

'Ja, mevrouw Royen. Hoe gaat het?' informeert de Thuiszorg zuster. 'Zat u wat te dutten?'

'U rukt me wel weer terug naar de realiteit.'

'O, hoezo?'

Ik zal haar de foto maar laten zien. Mijn dochter heeft die een aantal weken geleden gevonden en weer op de kast gezet. 'Ernst, heette hij. Misschien had ik mijn hele leven wel in Duitsland gewoond.' De zuster bekijkt de foto. Het zegt haar niets.

'Als de oorlog voorbij is, zien we elkaar weer.' De oorlog is allang voorbij, maar Ernst is nooit teruggekomen.

~.~

# *Forbidden Love*

*H*e had to go to the Eastern Front, my Ernst. It was at a
time when being involved with a German, and a German
soldier at that, was frowned upon. Years later, I married, I
had to. I was already four months pregnant when I got
married. To a Dutchman, a kind man and handsome, too,
but after our five children were born, he started drinking.
And no weak tea, mind. He had a taste for alcohol. He
didn't grow old with it. By then, we were already
separated. No, I did not want a divorce because if you
marry, it is for better and for worse.

But what would my life have been like if I had had the
chance to share it with Ernst? He was such a sweet boy,
but it was impossible at the time. After the war, images
came to light, of Dutch women whose heads were shaved
and they were ridiculed for having been involved with
Germans.

My father was not happy when he found out I had a
thing for a German soldier. I secretly saw Ernst, he was
sweet and we were in love, but there was a war, and then
he had to go to the Eastern Front. He gave me a photo, the
one that showed him with his dog. Just a handsome young
man with no trace of war around him. 'Von deinen lieben
Ernst' it says on the back. I had that picture on my bedside
table for years. A black and white memory of my love.

I can still see him leave. At the time, I was working as
a domestic worker for the local doctor, and I was standing
on the balcony when Ernst and an army friend headed for
the train station at the end of that street. We waved. I
waved until his blond head of hair was out of sight. He
sent me some lovely letters. But suddenly they stopped

coming.

'When I'm still alive, I'll come back to you, and then we will marry,' he had said. But I heard nothing. Had that, what I had feared, happened? Had he been killed on the Eastern Front?

When the war is over, we will meet again. The war was over, and I met Jan. I continued my life with him …

'Oh, are you here already?'

'Yes, Mrs Royen. How are you?' the Home Care Nurse asks. 'Were you snoozing?'

'You have pulled me back to the reality.'

'Oh, how so?'

I'd better show her the photograph. My daughter found it a few weeks ago and put it back on the cupboard.

'Ernst was his name. Maybe I would have lived in Germany all my life.' The Nurse looks at the photograph. It doesn't mean a thing to her.

'When the war is over, we will meet again.' The war is long gone, but Ernst never came back.

~.~

# *Murder*

'*Y*ou are always rather creative, dear,' Albert tells his wife, 'where shall we put the Christmas tree?' He walks about the large living room of his father's country estate, Glendale House, where all the children of old Frederick Godwin have gathered.

'Where it always is, darling,' his wife Louisa replies somewhat bored. She takes another sip from her dry sherry.

'Yes, but … In the hall. Not a good spot, now that the whole family has gathered. I think the dining room is best,' Albert says. He glances into his empty sherry glass.

'Whatever you say, darling,' Louisa replies.

'Why do you bother about that ridiculous Christmas tree!' Gerard cries out irritably. 'The old man doesn't care less about Christmas. It's all the same to him if the house is decorated or not!'

Startled, Brooke looks up from her magazine.

'It's Christmas, let's try and make it a nice one. Father will certainly have good reason to call us all here. Maybe he wants to make up for something,' Albert says.

'Good lord! How naive someone can be!' his wife exclaims.

'You'd be better off asking yourself *why* we all had to come here,' Gerard says. 'And why did the old man ask that good-for-nothing Dudley to come too?'

'Oh, he won't come,' Albert says. 'He's probably locked up somewhere. Again.'

'Don't be too sure about that,' Louisa says. 'If there is something to be gained, he's always there.'

'What do you mean *if there is something to be*

*gained*?' Albert enquires. 'You know to whom Father has pledged the lion share.'

Gerard expresses his displeasure with a hard slap on the desk. An act that makes the rest of the family look in his direction with discontent.

'And Gerard gets the crumbs, hey, Albert! Is that what you want to say?!' Gerard shouts.

Brooke gets up and paces towards her husband. 'Come now, you won't achieve anything by showing such behaviour, Gerard. Stay calm.'

Annoyed, Gerard pushes her aside and attempts to run towards Albert. His head is red with anger.

'Darling, please,' says Brooke, pulling Gerard's arm.

'You have nothing to worry about, Gerard,' Albert says. 'You are already well looked after. Father has seen to that. Mister politician,' he adds cynically.

'I'm warning you,' Gerard threatens, his finger raised.

'Come, come,' Louisa says soothingly. 'Don't make such a fuss.'

She turns when she notices the butler who has just entered. 'Yes, Osbourne?'

'Mr Dudley, Madam,' Osbourne politely introduces. Albert's face becomes tense.

'So he has come,' Gerard hisses through his teeth.

Dudley appears in the doorway and looks around the room. Then he walks over to Albert, smiling broadly. 'Well, little brother, how are you?' Dudley stretches out one hand to shake Albert's and with the other slaps him jovially on the shoulder. Albert can't do anything but shake the outstretched hand, albeit reluctantly.

'Gerard! Still in politics?'

'As if you care,' Gerard says.

Dudley shrugs and then approaches the ladies. 'And how are my favourite sisters-in-law?' he asks, kissing

Louisa on her hand and he gives Brooke a furtive wink. He turns away from them, saying: 'Well, as always, the welcome is overwhelming.'

'Why did you come, Dudley?' Gerard asks, glancing disapprovingly at the clothes his brother wears.

Dudley looks at him and pretends not to understand. 'It's almost Christmas. The whole family comes together. For sociable reasons, wouldn't you say? And because Father asked me to come, of course,' he adds bluntly.

' ... Do you, uh ... have any idea why?' Albert inquires.

Dudley shrugs his shoulders. 'Family matter?'

Albert and Gerard look at each other, unable to think of anything in these dubious circumstances.

'Well. Shall we have another drink?' Louisa suggests and rings the bell for Osbourne.

Old Frederick has taken a seat in his armchair, he scours the room until he lets his angry eyes rest on his offspring. 'What have I ever done to deserve such idlers as sons,' he growls.

'Maybe it's the upbringing?' Dudley offers.

Old Frederick's walking stick hits the floor with a harsh blow. 'Shut up!' he roars. 'Jailbird! Freeloader! You only came because you thought there is money to be had!'

'Well, Father,' Dudley replies, 'coincidentally, I was also interested in the ups and downs of my family.'

'What poppycock!' Gerard expresses.

'Sorry? And you did come to see the family?' Dudley wants to know.

'Silence!' roars old Frederick again. 'You only listen to what *I* have to say!' The old man sighs a heavy sigh and calms down a bit. 'You, Gerard, you have been a politician for some time now. I assume you've earned a pretty penny. So, I have decided to cut your allowance, which I think you never needed in the first place.'

'But, Father … ' Gerard is stunned.

'You live beyond your means, Gerard!' The old man bellows again. 'It is time you did something about that slut of a wife of yours. She spends all my money on the most nonsensical things … ' The vocal cords of old Frederick Godwin no longer seem to be able to bear such violence. He suddenly has a coughing fit. Trembling, he reaches for the glass on the side-table next to him.

'Let me help you,' Albert offers. Old Frederick's stick, however, stops him.

'Go away, I'm not an invalid, you hear!' he calls out.

He takes a long gulp of the liquid that burns in his throat. 'Aah, that's better,' he says with satisfaction. He stretches his back. 'Well, as you may have gathered, I was thinking about changing my will, but I'm not quite sure how. You three have never meant much to me. Oh, when you were little it was different, of course, but as grown men, you have performed very little. Looking back, you have only wasted my fortune.'

'But Father, you always said that my managing the estate was enough,' Albert protests.

'Damn it, Albert!' the old man roars again. 'Naive weakling! See what I made of my life … *and* I managed the estate!'

He turns to Dudley. 'We'd better keep quiet about you. You only tainted my reputation with your scam practices.'

'I just followed in your footsteps, Father, that's all,' Dudley reasons.

Bang! The stick hits the floor again.

'NEVER have I behaved like you!' Frederick roars. 'You won't get a penny from me anymore! Get out of my sight! Out of my sight, all of you! Out!'

Bewildered, the three sons make their way to the door.

'Albert!' Frederick calls out. 'I still have a bone to pick with you! Come here!'

Albert walks towards his father, uncertain for not knowing what is required of him.

'You can indeed manage the estate,' Frederick says in a loud voice, 'but only when I guide you. You can't manage anything on your own. What if I'm dead? Have you ever thought about that?! No, no, you're not fit at all to run my estate,' he says, shaking his head.

Albert looks at him, panicked. 'But, Father! I only did what I thought – '

'Thinking … is something you'd best not do, Albert,' Frederick says gruffly, 'for then, everything goes wrong. No, my decision stands. I'm selling the estate.'

'Father!'

'I haven't yet decided what I will do with the money. I still have to discuss that with my solicitor.'

'But Father! This is our house! Our home! We grew up here! You can't just – '

'Quiet! My decision is made, and now get out.'

Rendered speechless, Albert walks out of the room, defeated. He enters into the room next door where he finds the others. His perplexed face evokes questions and Gerard is the first to react. 'Has he cut you off?' is his ironic response.

Albert gives him a bland look. 'Don't joke about it.'

'So, what happened?' Dudley is curious to know.

'He's selling the estate.'

'What?' Gerard is astounded.

'He can't do that!' Dudley calls out.

Brooke and Louisa look on in amazement. 'Well, maybe it's for the best,' Brooke says. 'Then the money from the sale can be divided equally.'

'Don't be so damn stupid, woman,' is Gerard's annoyed response. 'The old man is not going to give us anything! Damn miser.'

'Oh, now you're calling Father a miser? After all that money he has given you through the years,' Dudley says. 'Unappreciative little bastard.'

Gerard makes to fly at him and his fist almost hits Dudley's face, but Albert interferes. 'Stop that! This is not a time to fight. Father is serious.'

The brothers look at each other.

'What happens now?' Gerard wants to know. 'Are we all to be left beggars?'

Albert looks indecisive. 'He can't say ... what will happen to the money.'

'He can't say, or he won't say,' Dudley says.

'This will not do!' Gerard calls out. 'We are entitled to that money! The old man won't live much longer. We are entitled to inherit his money!'

'Greedy bastard,' Dudley tells his brother. 'You've had so much already, and still you want more!'

'Please!' This time it is Louisa who objects. 'Stop that!' The others look in her direction.

'Let's have dinner. Afterwards, we can try and talk to Father,' she says. 'And find out what his plans are.'

By the time dessert was served, old man Godwin had gone to his room. He would not admit it, but he was tired and his nurse had helped him upstairs. There has hardly been time for good conversation during dinner, but presently the rest of the family look at each other with dubious glances.

'Maybe we should call Father's solicitor,' Gerard says.

Dudley waves the remark aside. 'It won't change anything if we do.'

'Yes, but then at least we would know,' Gerard replies. 'Then, we would have certainty.'

Albert gives him a scrutinizing look. 'And then what? What if we find out that Father leaves all his money to a charity. What good will that knowledge do us?'

'A charity?' is Gerard's surprised response. 'Don't be ridiculous. Father is the least charitable person on this earth!'

'There is a possibility,' Dudley offers.

Louisa looks at Brooke, who is finishing her pudding, pretending not to be interested in the arguments that the brothers display.

'Possibility ... Poppycock,' Gerard says. 'The old man would rather throw his money in the sea than let any charity have it. You don't know him.'

'And you do?' Dudley questions. 'You are just afraid that you'll come away empty-handed!'

'Please,' Louisa tries to calm the situation. 'Let's not speculate. There will be something for everybody.'

'You seem to be pretty sure about it,' Gerard addresses his sister-in-law. 'Is there something he has told you that we don't know about?'

'Of course not,' Louisa says. 'I don't know anymore than you do. I'm just saying ... that the chance we will all inherit, is there.'

Gerard is not convinced. He jumps up from his chair and paces out of the room. Silence sets in until Albert addresses his wife Louisa. 'I think we should turn in also, dear,' and he stands up to take his wife by her arm. Brooke follows them behind, leaving Dudley by himself at the table. He motions Osbourne to pour him another drink and then dismisses the butler. Dudley gets up and walks over to the fireplace. He leans on the mantelpiece and stares into the flames and takes a gulp from his brandy.

It was the nurse who found him. She went into Frederick Godwin's room and saw the pillow covered in blood and the old man on the floor beside his bed. His dead eyes wide open and staring at her. She screamed until Albert came out into the hall. He had a hard time trying to calm the woman. The nurse couldn't utter a word and just pointed to the old man's room.

'Louisa!' Albert called out. 'Louisa!' His wife came running in her dressing gown. 'Take her down,' her husband said. 'She's hysterical.'

Presently, Glendale is overrun by policemen from the village. By the entrance to the house, detective Belker is taking in the surroundings of the large property.

'Belker! What are you doing here?' Chief Inspector Gibbons calls out when he sees the detective.

'Special mission,' Belker replies with a grin. 'There seems to be quite a bit of money involved.'

'Weren't you in Spain?'

'Yes, yesterday,' Belker says. 'No rest for the wicked, I'm afraid. Where's the victim?'

'Brace yourself. It's not a pretty sight. The owner, Frederick Godwin, was found with a slit throat.'

'Mm … Merry Christmas,' Belker says. His glance wanders to a pretty woman, standing not far from them. 'John, who is that lady over there?'

'That's Louisa Godwin, the victim's daughter-in-law,' the Chief Inspector replies.

'Any other relatives present?'

'Oh yes, three sons and another daughter-in-law. Nobody was particularly fond of the victim.'

Belker nods and runs a hand through his unruly curls. 'OK. I'll see you in a moment,' he says.

He finds Louisa Godwin staring ahead of her to then continue attending to her rockery.

'Mrs Godwin?' Belker asks. 'My name is Belker, private detective.'

Louisa looks at him with a blank expression. 'How many policemen are working on this ... I'm sorry,' she says as she hides her face in her hands when she starts to cry.

'It's alright, Mrs Godwin,' Belker says.

Louisa searches for her handkerchief. 'I've been questioned by the police a few times ... I ... I don't know anything.'

Belker looks around. He notices how tasteful this part of the garden looks. 'Beautiful garden,' he says.

'Do you think so? I built it, a hobby of mine,' she says with a faint smile. With care, Belker touches some flowers that grow between the boulders. 'Very nice. When I ever retire I'd like to focus more on gardening, it has always interested me.'

Louisa's face brightens a little.

'Do you live here at Glendale?' Belker asks.

'Yes, ever since I married Albert.'

'Albert?'

'Albert Godwin, Frederick's son,' Louisa clarifies. 'Mr Belker, you have to understand, my father-in-law was not an easy person, but still, the way he met his end ... You don't wish that on your worst enemy.'

'No, of course not,' Belker says. His attention is drawn to a few glistening pebbles between the boulders in the rockery. He squats and takes a few in his hand.

'The pebbles are from Scandinavia. Aren't they beautiful?' Louisa says. 'From the mountains.'

'Certainly beautiful. Can I take one as a souvenir?'

Louisa smiles. 'Of course. Mr Belker, come with me, I'll introduce you to the rest of the family.'

Together they walk into the house where Belker looks up at the decorated domed ceiling. He is full of admiration and doesn't notice the police officer. 'I'm sorry,' Belker apologizes when he almost bumps into the policeman.

'Not to worry, Sir. Uh ... you are?'

'Belker, private detective.'

'Is that so.' The policeman scrutinizes him from top to bottom. 'My name is Harker, I'm working on this case and we don't need the help of a private detective, Mr Belker.'

'I'm here in a professional capacity,' says Belker. 'Imposing estate, don't you think?'

Harker looks at him. 'Whatever you say,' he says, 'but I don't have time to admire the grandeur of this estate. There is work to be done. If you want to excuse me.'

'But of course,' Belker says. He watches officer Harker walk out of the hall with a heavy stride.

Belker looks about him and sees Louisa Godwin enter the lounge room; he follows her there.

'Albert,' Louisa addresses her husband. 'This is detective Belker.'

'Another police officer?' Albert asks, somewhat surprised.

'No, not really, I work alone,' Belker replies.

'Where are the others?' Louisa wonders.

'Dudley is upstairs, I think. Gerard is talking to the Chief Inspector and Brooke has locked herself in her room,' and facing Belker, 'Brooke is rather upset, you see, such a violent act.'

'I'll see how she is,' Louisa says and leaves the room.

'Can you please show me where your father ... died?'

Belker asks Albert.

'Yes. Fine. Please, follow me.'

'You have two more brothers, I understand?' Belker asks as they go upstairs.

'Yes, officially, but Father could never resist bragging about all his illegitimate children. God knows where they all live ... and if they exist at all! Father has travelled a lot, you see. He wasn't a good husband, or Father. I don't understand why Mother stayed with him all these years.'

They arrive on the landing. Belker looks puzzled at the man who meets them there. Where has he seen that face before?

'This is Dudley,' Albert says.

'The black sheep of the family,' Dudley adds. 'I'm going to the village, it is getting too crowded here with all these policemen,' he says and goes down the stairs.

Old Frederick Godwin's corpse still lies on the floor where the nurse first saw him. He has been covered with a sheet.

'If you want to excuse me,' Albert says. He turns his head away from the crime scene.

'Yes, yes, of course,' Belker replies, half in thought.

He sits down on the windowsill and looks around the room. Two police officers are busy mapping the scene of the crime.

'Is anything missing?' Belker asks one of them.

'The safe was robbed, said to be full of diamonds.' He looks up from his task and sees that Belker is not in uniform. Are you from a newspaper or something?'

'No, I'm de ... uh, a colleague of the Chief Inspector.' Belker's eyes fall on a portrait above the fireplace.

'Astounding,' he says in a soft voice. 'That must be Frederick Godwin in his younger years.' One of the policemen looks in his direction and follows Belker's gaze towards the painting. 'Spitting image of Dudley Godwin.'

He walks over to the body and lifts the sheet. The pool of blood under the dead man's head has darkened and dried. The neck is completely covered in blood, it is almost impossible to see where he was cut. The old man's left hand, now resting on his chest as if frozen, is also covered in blood. The clean, right hand lies clenched next to the body.

'Mm,' Belker mumbles. He strokes his chin and tries to imagine how the man must have reacted just before death struck. Grabbing his neck? But why only with his left hand? In an attempt to put himself in the dead man's situation, Belker slides his left hand to his own throat while he clenches his right hand into a fist. He then kneels beside the body and tries to open the already stiff right hand.

'Ah, Belker, there you are,' the Chief Inspector's voice sounds behind him. Belker doesn't answer, he has just managed to open the old man's hand. He takes out a button with a small piece of blue fabric attached to it. The inspector looks over Belker's shoulder. 'Good lord,' is his surprised reaction.

'Indeed,' Belker responds. He drops the find in a clean handkerchief and hands it to the Chief Inspector.

'Oh,' Belker remembers, 'while you send that off to the lab, you might want to have this checked also.' He reaches in his pocket and takes out the pebble he took from the rockery.

'Any other findings?' Belker asks the inspector.

'We've questioned the family. They all seem to have an alibi.'

'There are two married couples, Sir. They *would* give each other alibi's.'

'True. And they all had motive, too.'

Belker gives him a questioning look.

'Frederick Godwin was in the process of selling the estate,' the Chief Inspector says.

'And the proceeds?' Belker asks.

'Only he knew that.' He nods towards the dead man, 'None of the sons was a favourite of their father. He might've left all his money to a stranger, had he been given the chance.' He gives Belker a meaningful look. 'There is quite a bit of friction among the siblings.'

'Ah, so one of them could've killed the father, to prevent the sale,' Belker says.

The Chief Inspector shrugs his shoulders. 'Who is to say? But, we can't speculate, Belker. We want facts!' And he holds up the items that Belker just handed to him. The two police officers in the room have finished and leave with Chief Inspector Gibbons. A few minutes later the people from the funeral home enter and Belker decides to continue his investigating elsewhere in the house.

The following day around noon, the phone in the hall at Glendale rings and Belker's name is called. He'd come back to tie up some loose ends at the scene of the murder. A moment later, he appears and takes the telephone from Osbourne. Belker learns it's Chief Inspector Gibbons on the other end of the line. 'Sir,' Belker says. 'And? Was it a match?'

'*An exact match*,' the inspector replies. '*You were right, Belker.*' The Chief Inspector sounds triumphant.

'Good,' Belker says. 'How soon can you get here?'

'*I'm on my way.*'

In the large reception room, the Godwin family has gathered, supervised by three police officers, including Harker, when Belker and the Chief Inspector are shown in by Osbourne.

'Why the mystery?' Gerard asks angrily. 'We are guarded here like a bunch of criminals. While you should be tracking down the killer!'

Belker looks at him calmly. 'That has already been done, Mr Godwin,' he says.

Gerard doesn't understand. 'But what are you still doing here then?'

'Because the killer is here,' and after a short pause. 'It's one of Frederick Godwin's sons who did it.'

The three brothers look at one other. Brooke shrieks, Louisa can't utter a word.

'Have you gone mad?' Albert calls out. 'We were not very fond of Father, but we would never kill him!'

'You all had a motive,' Belker says in a loud voice and he slowly walks across the room. He stops in front of Dudley.

'Please!' Dudley calls out. 'What do you take us for!'

'Harker!' Belker calls out. Harker walks over to Dudley and grabs his arm.

'Let me go, you idiot!' the struggling Dudley shouts.

'Harker, Harker,' Belker says soothingly, shaking his head.

Harker loosens his grip on Dudley while Belker walks around the men and then stands between them.

'Does anyone notice anything about these gentlemen?' Belker asks.

'Stop this playing around!' Gerard calls out in anger and to Dudley: 'You, you ... I would never have thought you could do such a thing!'

'Me! Have you gone mad!' Dudley shouts.

'Gentlemen!' Belker calls out to calm them. He looks around the room. 'What would officer Harker look like without that nice big moustache?'

'This is crazy!' Albert says. He is starting to lose his patience.

Belker continues unperturbed. 'If officer Harker wouldn't have such a nice big moustache, he would bear a striking resemblance to ... Dudley.'

'But ... Sir,' Harker utters.

Everyone in the room turns their face towards Harker.

'Yes, but ... ' Albert begins.

Louisa looks at Brooke in disbelief, then gazes at Harker, who looks perplexed.

'You don't mean officer Harker ... This is madness!' Gerard says incredulously.

'Of course it is,' officer Harker says. 'He's crazy!'

Belker has to contradict him. 'Officer Harker is indeed a Godwin.' He walks over to the Chief Inspector. 'Sir?'

The inspector reaches in his inside pocket and takes out a sheet of paper. 'Here's the birth certificate,' Chief Inspector Gibbons says, and reads, 'William, boy, born in Allyth. Mother, Mary Elizabeth Harker. Father ... Frederick Godwin.'

A surge of disbelief and indignation sweeps through the room.

'Isn't it true that old Frederick Godwin used to go to Scotland? To hunt?' the Chief Inspector continues. Harker looks at the inspector with a startled face.

'Yes, Harker, we just found this in a house search. Your house. And another thing that might interest you, a blue shirt. You know, the one with the missing button?'

Harker's face darkens.

'Belker found that button in the hand of the deceased,' Chief Inspector Gibbons says.

The Godwin family is surprised and horrified at the same time. Albert's mouth falls open, but he is lost for words.

'That … that doesn't prove anything!' Harker calls out.

'The shirt you wore when you cut old Frederick's throat!' Belker says in a loud voice. Harker turns pale.

At that moment, Brooke faints and falls to the floor. Louisa rushes over to her and bends down to attend to her sister-in-law. Gerard is unsure whether he should punch Harker or worry about his wife.

'Why?' Albert utters. 'Why on earth would want to kill our father? What has he ever done to you?'

Harker's face turns cold. 'He was a selfish bastard! He was – '

'Hold on! That's a family matter!' Gerard cries out. 'Who are you to criticise our father?'

'Look who's talking,' Dudley says.

'You're all a bunch of hypocrites!' Harker says. 'You hated him just as much as I did!'

The brothers look at each other for the defamation of this stranger.

'But my mother and I knew something you didn't know,' Harker continues. 'We are sole heirs to all this!' Triumphantly he looks around the room.

'What! You bloody liar!' Gerard calls out.

'So, you see, I had to kill him,' Harker continues. 'We couldn't allow him to make changes to that will.'

The Godwin brothers look at each other in disbelieve. Gerard is quite taken aback. He addresses Albert.

'Does this mean that … *his* mother will now get our home?' he says in a soft tone. Dudley rolls his eyes.

'Not if I can help it,' Albert replies decidedly.

Louisa, who has just helped Brooke to a chair, looks at her husband. 'I won't accept a stranger living in our house!'

'Of course not,' Albert replies.

Belker is not completely satisfied. 'Why did you take the diamonds from the safe?' he asks Harker.

'Oh, that. Shame really, I should've kept them. Mother would've loved those.'

The Chief Inspector shakes his head and indicates for the two policemen to arrest their colleague Harker. 'One thing is certain, Harker, you won't get much enjoyment out of your inheritance,' he says.

Harker looks at him with a grin on his face as he is handcuffed.

'The theft of those diamonds was probably to throw us off the scent. Right, Harker?' Belker says. 'Make it look like a burglary?'

'Clever man!' Harker says over his shoulder as he is led away.

The Godwin family view the scene with incredulous faces. 'The impertinence!' Albert calls out.

'May he rot in hell!' Gerard grants.

'At least we can now start mourning our father,' Dudley says.

'Oh, for Christ's sake. You *are* a hypocrite,' Gerard concludes.

Chief Inspector Gibbons and Belker look out of the window and watch the policemen in the forecourt as they escort the murderer into the police van.

~.~

# Hitch~hiker

At mid-day, the sun burned inexorably on the asphalt. She'd been standing by the side of the road for a few hours and impatience started to torment her. She pulled her straw hat a little further over her eyes and raised her thumb again. Finally, an approaching car slowed down. A man with a child. He stopped a few meters away from her.

'Are you going to Auckland?' she asked through the open car window.

'Yeah. Well, most of the way. Hop in,' and to the child, 'let the lady in, Joey.'

'Thank you,' she said. She threw her backpack in the back seat and took place next to it.

'What's your name?' he asked as he hit the accelerator. She noticed that he was looking in the rearview mirror. To her surprise, she was shocked when his eyes met hers. 'Oh, ... er ... Yvonne.'

'Nice name,' he said. 'I'm Jim and this is my son Joey. Are you on vacation?'

'Yes. Well, backpacking. I've been here three months now,' she said. She sat slightly diagonally behind him and saw his slim, tanned hands on the steering wheel. He looked sideways to point out a distant house to his son.

She admired his nice profile and his dark hair that curled slightly where it met the frayed hem of his jeans shirt. Her eyes slid from his smooth cheek to his arms, which protruded from the rolled-up sleeves and rested on the fingers playing on the wheel. Suddenly she heard the music that sounded from an invisible speaker. Had the music been playing all the time? She couldn't remember.

'I can take you to the next junction. Is that okay with

you?' she suddenly heard his voice say. Quickly, she looked up, straight into those beautiful, dark eyes of the rearview mirror.

'Uh … Yes, fine.'

'Have you been in Auckland before?'

'Yes,' she said, 'But … Only for two days.'

'Wait,' he said. He reached into the glove compartment, took out a matchbox and gave it to her. 'A friend of mine owns that bar. Very sociable place. Many people like you go there.'

'Oh, thank you.'

Before she realized, she stood on the sandy bank by the roadside.

'You have to follow that road,' his voice echoed. He had pointed to the right. He had turned left.

She looked out the window of her room in the guest house and saw the Travellers Bar just down the street. The matchbox played through her fingers. She looked at it again. Travellers Bar, 28 Mount Eden road. His friend was the owner. The half-empty box had to mean that he came there regularly. Why had he given it to her? Did he want to meet her? Without arousing the child's suspicion? Children simply pass everything on to their mothers.

As she glanced up at the clock above the bar, she concluded it was half past nine. It was a fun place; he'd been right about that. Many like-minded people too. But he hadn't shown up, yet.

She kept hoping he would appear and was about to sit down when she heard her name called.

'Hello, Yvonne … '

She felt joy as she turned around.

'Oh, hi,' was her disappointing response when she

looked Craig in his face. She had spent a few days with him on the South Island.

'Also back from the front?'

'Yes,' she replied.

'Here, have a drink on me, we have something to celebrate.'

She looked at him quizzically.

'We made it!' Craig said. 'We're back in Auckland.'

Craig always found ways to make simple things sound extraordinary.

False light was thrown into the bar when the door opened for the umpteenth time. He had come after all.

She mindlessly accepted Craig's drink and smiled slightly. 'Sorry Craig, I'll see you later.'

She went over and stood next to *him* at the bar.

'My woman had to go to her mother's, I'll pick her up later,' she overheard him say to the bartender.

Then, he turned his head. 'Oh, hello,' he said, surprised. 'You found it.'

She felt her face turn red and felt at a loss as to what to say. 'I just wanted to thank you for the lift,' she quickly said.

He made an indistinct gesture with his hand. 'Anytime, anytime.'

Before she knew it, she said: 'A friend is waiting for me. Bye.'

His dark eyes followed her as she walked back to Craig.

She sat by the window in her room and looked out into the darkness. The Travellers Bar's neon light had long been turned off. It was three o'clock in the morning. A few more days, then her flight would take her back to where she belonged. She didn't want to leave.

She couldn't sleep. He had a *woman* and a child. If the woman was his wife, he would have said so.

It was not too late. She could still try and contact him. No, no, what was she thinking? He was happy in his world. She had no right. She looked towards the Travellers Bar once more, then she got up. She started looking through her papers for the airline's phone number.

Seven days had passed and her planned flight home had left five days before. On every one of those days, she had visited the Travellers Bar, for lunch and dinner and sociable evenings with her fellow travellers. For most of those travellers, the journey had come to an end and they had made it to the airport. She never told them what kept her in the country. She persisted and was adamant to meet the man who had given her a ride on, what should have been, one of her last days in this country. Staff at the Travellers Bar had sometimes jokingly remarked that she was part of the furniture.

As she ordered yet another meal, she noticed a photograph above the bar that hadn't been there before. On closer inspection, she saw that the man in the photo was Jim. Standing next to him was a woman in a wedding dress.

Her shocked stare at the photograph drew the attention of the young man who was serving her.

'Something wrong?' he asked.

Bewildered she looked at him. 'No. Yes. The man in that photo, I know him.'

'Really?' He seemed surprised.

'Who is that woman with him?' she asked.

'My sister-in-law,' he replied.

She felt some sort of peculiar relief.

'That's my brother in that picture,' he then said with

pride. 'He got married a few days ago, thought I'd stick his wedding photo up there. As he was a regular here.' He looked at her with a broad smile on his face.

The relief she'd felt seconds before was swept away. She staggered out of the Travellers Bar and into the street where she leaned against a tree.

'Yvonne!'

She did not react.

'Yvonne! Are you still here?' Craig approached her. 'Are you all right?'

She turned his way. 'Oh. Hi.'

'I thought you'd left days ago,' he said.

She didn't know what to say and she was not in the mood to admit to the reason why she had cancelled her flight.

'Say, as you're still here, why not come with me around the East Cape?'

She looked at him. 'Not sure, Craig. I'm low on money. I should go home.'

'Get a job. Fruit picking season starts soon,' Craig said. 'We can go together.'

She looked about her and to the Travellers Bar; suddenly a meaningless building. 'Fine,' she said and she walked away towards the guest house where she still stayed.

~.~

# Tree Wisdom

*F*ive hundred and thirty-five years ago on this spot, a chestnut fell from a tree. The space next to me where my parent once stood from which that chestnut must have fallen, has long been empty and it is covered with indistinct plants and grass. When I wriggled myself out of the chestnut as a youngster and started my life as a young plant, many trees grew all over. But, as I grew closer and closer to heaven, my relatives disappeared around me. Storms sometimes caused the oldest trees to bend so far down that they snapped and there was no stopping it. Branches, canopies and trunks fell to the ground and were swallowed up by the earth. Sometimes my relatives also disappeared because of that annoying species that walk on *two* trunks and are constantly in motion. They would come here with hatchets and murder my family. Their death throes during those massacres were ignored. That has always hurt me a lot. Suddenly, bald spots where just moments before an uncle or cousin stood; that's heavy to bear. In subsequent storms, the winds had free rein and the old trees who had endured for hundreds of years were blown down to earth. I never liked the loss of friends and family because, apart from good company, I lost a lot of peers with whom I could have a good conversation.

Now and then a small tree started to sprout from the earth at my feet and grew, and so potential interlocutors appeared in that way. But, actually, I feel more of a parent than an equal then.

You simply cannot have in-depth conversations with those youngsters. They are just ogling each other. Look over there, that Oak, he gets along very well with the

Beech standing next to him. Fortunately, a few meters away from me, another tree grows that I have known since *I* took root here. I have long conversations with that forest giant, especially when the wind is blowing hard. I have to raise my voice because the beautiful old giant is getting a little deaf. Recently there was a huge storm and suddenly there was a flash. My buddy, that old forest giant, lost a thick branch in one fell swoop. Now there is a bare spot at the top of his canopy. Flutterers have found a home there now.

I enjoy it when it is warm, then it looks beautiful here with us. But, it has been cold here recently and we were looking straight through each other. Fortunately, I feel a tickle in my branches again and small shoots are becoming visible.

It will be warm again soon.

~.~

# Smart phone

*I*n the darkness of a rainy evening, a floating bright light from a smartphone is the only indication that someone is moving along. Someone on a bicycle, moving along in the dark street. The small bright light illuminates a face. The person is busy talking, letting the oncoming cars light the way. Only a floating bright light is visible where the street becomes quiet.

Bernd is on his way home by train. The worst of the rush hour is over, and not all seats in the compartment are taken. Some passengers are dozing with their heads against the window, while others are preoccupied with their smartphones. There is not much opportunity to talk because everyone is busy communicating all kinds of issues via I-pad or smartphone. Everyone in their own world.

Bernd's smartphone vibrates and he looks at the display. It's a message from his fiancée. His fingers quickly start typing a message: 'Can't make calls now, I'll be home in 25 minutes.' The message is sent before a second has passed. Bernd has other things to do, his fingers are flying over the keys and message after message is sent into the air. Messages fly back and forth throughout the compartment. There is no time for a chat with other passengers, but digital communication is working overtime.

At the station, Bernd walks over to the Park 'n Ride, his phone to his ear: 'I just arrived, I'll be home in ten minutes.' He opens his car door and gets in. While he starts the car with one hand, he quickly sends a last message with the other. Then he throws his smartphone on the dashboard, in plain view so that he can see when it goes off. The rain demands that he switches on his windscreen wipers. He turns out of the parking area and merges with other traffic onto the shiny, wet road. He accelerates. The warm stove at home awaits. At the next intersection, he turns, while he sees the rain pouring down from the sky. From a distance, he perceives flashing lights, blue flashing lights. Through the veils of rain, he sees a police car and an ambulance, and he starts to slow down. A policeman indicates for him to stop. The street has been closed off, and a way forward is not possible. He looks back and sees that the cars behind him have stopped. He is stuck.

Slightly frustrated, he looks at the distorted scene through the pouring rain that streams down his window. He makes out a bicycle, completely bent, lying on the road. A stretcher on the street has a body on it. He reaches for his smartphone and dials his fiancée's number. She's not answering. Again he looks at the dreadful scene in front of him. The bent bicycle, the bicycle bag and the drenched items that lay beside it. His fiancée has a bicycle bag just like that.

Bernd warily opens the door and gets out of his car. He walks a little closer to the accident, but a policeman stops him. 'Please, be patient, Sir.'

When the stretcher is lifted onto its wheels, he sees it. His fiancée's bloodied head. 'Karen!' He passes the policeman. 'Sir!' the latter shouts and grabs Bernd by his arm. 'But, Karen. My fiancée.'

The policeman looks at him. 'Your fiancée? I'm sorry, Sir, but it doesn't look good.'

Bernd stares at him in disbelief. 'I have to go to her.'

He walks over to the stretcher that is placed in the ambulance.

'Karen!' He looks at the paramedics. 'What happened?'

'Sorry, Sir, step aside, she needs surgery as soon as possible.'

'I'll follow the ambulance to the hospital,' is all Bernd can say.

Dazed, he walks back to his car when his foot kicks something aside. It's a smartphone. When he picks it up, he sees that it is Karen's. 'Missed call' it says on the display.

~.~

# *Orange Wave in Stuttgart*
World Championships in Germany, 2006

*H*olland plays in Stuttgart, and naturally, the orange-clad fans are in on it. The fun and joy have started early. Stuttgart was prepared for everything. Not a single security measure has been ignored. During the World Cup, the Stuttgarter Strassen Bahnen[1] have adjusted the schedules. The police brought in reinforcements. Everything is ship-shape, after all this is Germany.

During the match against Ivory Coast, it soon became clear who would be the winner, and when the final whistle sounded at 8 pm the Dutch continued to rejoice.

No hard feelings from the opponent. Holland is satisfied. There's a contented, jubilant, cheerful atmosphere among the Dutch fans.

Fans who managed to purchase a ticket to the game at the Daimler Stadium on the north side of the river now move in a massive orange wave to the centre of town. 35.000 fans stream in an orange wave towards the fans' party, triumphantly chanting, orange mixes with orange. Some Dutchmen can't resist an organ grinder and circle around the man in polonaise. A flowing orange wave, moving up and down.

Palace Square is the venue where fans of different football clubs meet, and on this day the party has been in full swing since morning. It leaves little to the imagination as to who the predominant people are here today. One of the celebrations during the World Cup is a special *Weindorf* event that takes place from June through to July.

---

1 Public Transport

The fans already present at Palace Square, enjoy the pleasures of the new vintage. Here too, orange is the dominant colour. Some Dutchmen have found coolness in one of the large fountains at Palace Square -it's 30° C after all- and climbed up the statue, to the top.

And then there's this immense Dutch flag, the red-white-and-blue, completely soaked because of that fountain. What should you do with it? You roll it into a long, thick cord and use it as a skipping rope! Candidates a-plenty.

Where in some countries you'd be arrested on the spot for 'desecration of the flag' and perhaps end up in prison, as a Dutchman you just wash your flag so it can be reused at the next event. No man overboard. When the Dutch party, they party with a wink. The police, keeping an eye on the football fans, observe it all with a smile, and maybe in their hearts, they are a bit envious about the ease in which the Dutch can express themselves.

Orange remains a beautiful colour.

~.~

# *Refugee*

As she lets herself down on a bench at the edge of the forest, the storm starts to rise. First, the branches of the trees sway gently back and forth, but soon an unknown force tears at the branches, sweeping them to one side. Her dog, when not smelling any rabbits, usually walks along quietly, but now looks in her direction as if inquiring: 'Shouldn't we go back to our warm house?'

She leaves him be, rooting in the earth, looking for something unknown. She gets up and turns her face to the wind. Unstrained, she lets her thoughts wander to her convivial village, to the people who do their shopping in the small shops. Now, unquestionably, fighting against the wind, as they quickly make their way back to their homes. Homes. Accommodation. Warm and dry. How many people on this earth do not have these basic needs? She crawls a little deeper into her collar and pulls her scarf a little tighter. The wind tears at her hair. Inequality, dishonesty. She can't bear it. She has everything a person needs to live a normal life, while so many have to *survive*. She thinks about what it would do to her if she had to survive in an unfair situation. Would she accept it? Would she become aggressive?

She feels the first droplets of rain. If only she had put on her raincoat. 'Let's go,' she says and her dog immediately follows her. They take a path between trees that gives them the most shelter from the blowing wind. The rain is now hitting the forest path with large drops. She picks up her pace. Her dog has already gone ahead of her and occasionally looks back to see if she is still following him.

Suddenly, he stops when a dark figure blocks his way. He jumps aside and starts barking. She looks up and stops when she sees the figure. The dark-skinned man steps aside to avoid the threatening and barking dog. She sees the man's startled face and feels the need to apologize, but she keeps quiet. Her mistrust takes over.

'You dog?' but the storm blows the words into the wind.

'Sorry? Do you mean, if it's my dog?'

The man is clearly uncomfortable, but when he wants to walk away, her dog starts barking even more viciously. She approaches and calms him down. 'That's enough,' she tells the Dobermann.

'Dangerous, you dog. You have to hold it,' the man explains.

Her dog, a danger? Irritation wells up inside of her. 'Sorry, but dogs are allowed to roam freely in this part of the forest,' she says. She looks at the man who seems to have calmed down.

'Uh, can you help?' he asks. 'I lost way. Everything is same.'

Lost indeed, the man doesn't look like your average European. There is no asylum seekers centre in her village, and she knows there have been no new residents.

'Where do you need to go?' she asks him.

In broken English, the man begins to explain elaborately where he came from and how he must have lost his way. She becomes impatient because of the man's ways and the pouring rain. 'Just walk with us. We're going back to the village. The bus goes from there.'

'Bus?'

'Yes. How else did you get here?'

'I uh. I am ridden with someone.'

'You had a ride with someone?'

'Yes, ride.'

She wonders why she suggested showing the man the way back to the village, a total stranger. Fortunately, she has her dog with her.

'Thank you for help,' the man says. 'You see, I'm not in England very long. I don't know the way.'

'Where are you from?' she wants to know. She watches her dog run freely in front of them. He has let go of his mistrust.

'Far away,' says the man. 'Syria. Dangerous for people.'

'Do you have any family?'

It seems as if the man does not want to elaborate on his life. 'Everybody dead,' he then says. 'Dangerous in Syria.'

She is more or less aware of the situation in that region, through the media. War, refugees, but she doesn't know much else. It's all far away from her friendly village. And they prefer to spend their holidays in Switzerland or France. Yes, now and then the threat comes closer. A few weeks ago, just like that, hostages and murders in Paris. Last year she was in Paris with her husband. They enjoyed it very much. And now? Now she's walking here with a man she doesn't know at all. What is he up to? Is he genuinely looking for the way back to the village? Out of the corner of her eyes, she glances sideways, at his coat pockets where the man's fists are hidden. His face, half-covered by his collar.

The wind is pulling at the branches while the rain is only getting worse. The man ducks a little deeper into his collar. 'Bad weather,' he says. 'Cold.'

She turns into a side path, following her dog. 'In here,' she says. 'We are almost there.'

They follow the path when the first houses come into

view. She wonders whether the man might be a Muslim, lost in the Anglican UK. Muslims committed the attacks in Paris. She glances at the man, who doesn't look hostile. Maybe he's just a regular Christian from the Middle East. He feels her look at him and smiles at her.

They leave the last trees behind them and walk from the forest path up the pavement on the edge of the village.

'Ah, I see now,' the man says. 'This is where I walked.'

'Do you know where to go now?' she asks. 'Come on, I'll walk with you. The bus runs through the main street.'

The man looks at her again but says nothing. They walk through a narrow street, and a few shops come into view. Out of nowhere, a blonde woman suddenly approaches them. 'Amir!'

The man's face lights up.

'Amir! Where have you been?' She sounds relieved. 'I've been looking everywhere for you.'

'I was in woods. I said.'

'Do you know this man?' she asks the blonde woman as she takes her dog to put his leash back on.

'Yes, I'm his case worker. He wanted to go for a walk, but he'd just gone. I couldn't find him anywhere.'

'He was lost in the woods. So, he walked with me.'

'Oh, thank you very much for your help,' the woman says. 'Thank you so much. Is there anything we can do for *you*?'

'No, we have to get home. This awful weather all of a sudden.' She excuses herself and is about to move on.

'Come on, we'll treat you to a hot cup of coffee,' the blonde woman says decidedly. 'There is a nice tea-house over there.'

She doesn't know what to think of it, and she can afford a cup of coffee.

'Amir would also appreciate it,' says the blonde woman. The man nods.

Without further resistance, she allows herself to go with the two.

'He's had a terrible life,' the woman softly says. 'His whole family ... perished. That's why, nice people like you. It's good that there are nice people like you.'

Together they enter the tea house when Amir holds the door open.

~.~

# *Treasure*

*T*his bird. I'd never heard this song before. It wasn't a song, but this high-pitched cry: 'Aah', like someone blowing on a whistle. It had me in doubt first. Was it a bird? Was someone blowing a whistle? I had soon found that the high-pitched cry came from above, where the rooftops are. No one could possibly sit on a roof blowing on a whistle. Just one 'aah'! It must be a bird that recently moved into the area.

I had noticed my new neighbour moving into the upper apartment the week before. He looked like an odd bird himself. His furniture was battered and broken and ran the colours of the rainbow. The green sofa was missing a leg. The purple Ottoman looked lumpy, all the lamps were fringed. I couldn't look inside all the trunks and boxes he'd carried up but they looked old and well-travelled as if they came from some exotic locale. Could there have been a bird inside of one of them? What stories would it tell?

Another squeal broke the morning stillness. Then, a word: 'Treasure.'

Inquisitively I looked up at the upper apartment and opened my kitchen window. All of a sudden, a strange exotic bird fluttered down and sat on my window sill. It looked at me with these unfamiliar round little beads. These intense dark, black eyes were surrounded by green feathers, the rest of its small head was covered in tiny red feathers, his wings were a mixture of shiny dark blue, red and green feathers. With his cheeky beads of eyes, he looked at me as if expecting something, something to eat. I reached for the half tomato I'd just cut up to put on my sandwich and held it out in front of his greedy yellow beak. Before I could blink an eye he'd grabbed the piece of tomato and gobbled it down.

'Treasure!' it squalled. 'Yes,' I said, 'that is a treasure. I'm sure you won't get that every day.'

From then on he came to my window three times a day, with his ravenous appetite. It wasn't a problem for in those days I was still working in the corner market downstairs. Although I didn't admit this to my friends, the new bird from 'upstairs' did indeed have something to do with my moving uptown. I was getting unhealthily attached to 'Treasure' as I soon dubbed the bird. I never was one to keep pets, never had time, always working, but this bird with his beautiful coloured coating and high-pitched squeaks affected me greatly. The strange thing was, I hardly ever saw the odd man in the upper apartment who brought this bird into the neighbourhood, which had me wondering if dear old Treasure was ever being fed. Why would he otherwise always come to my window?

But I decided, it had to stop, I couldn't keep feeding this bird that wasn't even mine, so when the corner market downstairs moved its business elsewhere, I moved with it. Before I left my apartment I fed Treasure one more time, stroked his wings -he liked that- and moved to my new place uptown with a great view over a small park. As I stood there in front of the open window overlooking the park something fluttered down on my window sill. 'Treasure,' it squeaked and there I stared into those dark beady eyes again.

**by Caroline, Christine, Karin and Jim M.**

## Arranged marriage

*H*ere I am, sitting on a bench in a German town. My husband, as usual, sits away from me, with his friends. For the millionth time, I've cleaned the house. For the millionth time, we were at the store, grocery shopping. Most of which I had to carry to the car myself. My husband, in charge of the key, held open the boot so I could lift the heavy litre packs of apple juice and mineral water in there.

Oh, he helped, he always helps. He carried the toilet rolls and bags of crisps in the carrier-bag. Vegetables I always get at the market, nice and fresh. My husband likes it that way; he then waits in the café with his friends. They like smoking the water-pipe and drinking coffee. He says it's the only diversion he gets. I sometimes like to sit with them, some wives can, but my husband doesn't like that. He sees enough of me at home, he says.

My daughters, oh my daughters, thank God, I raised them in this country. My oldest is going to University now. Thank God, she refused to marry that horrible uncle of my brother-in-law. Ugly man. What is a beautiful young woman to do with a 58-year-old man? My husband didn't speak to my daughter for weeks. He said she had brought shame on the family. Thank God my daughters are smart and know what they want. They're not like my sons. My sons were always with their father. He showed them what a good man needs to know. He took them with him and showed them what *work* was. 'If you want good woman, you need good work' my husband always told them, 'Woman cost money, they want good house'. One of my sons is still in school. He wants to work for the Railways like his father, but he is too young. He has to finish school first. My other two sons couldn't work for the Railways after they had left school. They didn't need workers at the Railways. They now hang out with friends and go to the Job Centre when they feel like it. I told them to go to University, but my husband says University is not for strong men. 'They need work, strong man *work*, *not* sit in office', he always says.

My youngest daughter is now fourteen, she wants to be a doctor. My husband doesn't like it, 'she can only be woman doctor' he says. My daughter told him that that will keep her busy for a long time, for there are a lot of women in the world. My husband gets angry then and goes to the café and smokes the water-pipe and drinks coffee with the men.

I had dreams when I was young, I wanted to be a beautician. I was pretty then. My mother always told me I was a very pretty girl. But my father didn't want to hear of it, he had already arranged for me to marry the son of his friend. Before I knew it I had five children and I was fat. I'm still fat. Maybe it's a good thing that I wear loose clothes so nobody can see I don't have a waist. And maybe it's a good thing, too, that I have to wear a headscarf. That way it saves me having to buy dye for my hair. My hair is grey now. I started going grey when I was thirty-five. Thirty-five and grey and fat.

I had beautiful hair when I was young, it was long and black and it shone. My mother used to comb it for me. She always said how beautiful my hair was. My daughters have beautiful hair. My eldest has a boyfriend now. My husband doesn't know of course. We will tell him when the timing is right.

I never had a boyfriend. I had just turned sixteen when I had to show up at this wedding, that turned out to be my own. I still remember how my mother grieved and cried. Cried for me, for she knew about the dreams I had. That won't happen to me. If I cry at my daughter's wedding it will be of happiness, for my daughter will marry the one she wants and loves. I will see to that.

I'd better go. My youngest daughter will be home from school soon. I think I'll take the tram. My husband won't miss me anyway.

~.~

# *A Christmas Story*

At night the snow started to fall. At first, the silent flakes scattered across the countryside, landing softly on fences and trees, but soon they covered the green grass in a greyish blanket that shone blue by the light of the moon.

The winds came unexpectedly and soon the snow engulfed the fields in furious flurries. Animals that had still enjoyed the last rays of the autumn sun during the day, now stood gathered in small groups, close together with their backs to the icy wind that blew the fierce snow over the pastures. There, where accumulated soil kept the snow from drifting, it gathered into ever-increasing obstacles and formed into small mounds, giving the fields the appearance of frigid blankets with protruding white stones. The storm raged fiercely, trees bent over in its path. Snow could not settle there, but made heaps behind every tree where the snow could not escape. Through the icy blanket along a narrow road, two headlights appeared. First, it seemed the lights were a trick of the eye, but they came nearer, struggling against the incredible force of the winds that violently billowed over the countryside, and carried icy flakes with it. It was impossible to see with the naked eye what it was that made the headlights swiftly turn and come to an abrupt halt against a tree by the road, that by then, could not be distinguished from its surroundings. One could confuse the howling of the wind with the barely audible voice that cried out. A scarcely recognisable cry, silenced by the sound of the booming and wailing winds. Then, a figure emerged. It struggled to open the door of the vehicle and fought against the forces of the storm in this barbaric weather. The harsh wind swept the feeble cries for help in a distance, as it swept the snow over the fields. Bent against the fierce snowstorm, the figure moved like a shadow attempting to leave the site that was responsible for its predicament. The lonely shadow forced its way through the gruesome weather and slowly disappeared from view until dissolved by the sweeping snow sheets.

As outside the snowstorm raged, he lay peacefully in the hay and thought how lucky he had been to find this barn. After running away from the foster family a few days earlier, with only a few of his personal belongings, the blizzard had taken him by surprise. He had not walked along main roads but through fields and had to hide when cars approached, for he was afraid he might be caught and sent back to that house. He had started running down a road through an area unknown to him. After following the country road, with the snow beating against his face, and hardly able to perceive the surroundings, he had practically bumped into this barn. He could stay here as long as he liked. There was still some food in his bag, and no one would look for him there. A smile slid across his young face.

'I'm free now,' he murmured and closed his eyes.

It was the quietness in the morning that woke him. He turned his head and had to blink against a stream of light that shone directly on his face. As he rose from his hay bed, he took in his surroundings. The barn was large. In one corner was a rusty machine; possibly once used for agriculture. Other than that, it was just him and the hay. He slid to the ground and searched for the door through which he had entered in the dark of night. When he reached it, he pushed it against the weight of the snow that had gathered before the door. After one last push, the door moved, giving him enough room to climb the pile of snow in front of it. The weather had cleared, and the sun was shining in a stark blue sky. He reached down and put a handful of snow into his mouth; he was thirsty. The white flakes that melted in his mouth were icy cold, but it didn't bother him. He looked up at the sun and the surrounding countryside that spread such peacefulness as if nothing had battered its fields and trees in the night. He started running and laughing, grabbing the snow and throwing it over his head, enjoying every moment of his newfound freedom. He laughed as he ran down the forest lane and back again to his safe haven.

Suddenly he stopped in his tracks. In front of him, the snow had formed a small mound, higher than anything else around it. He saw a piece of cloth sticking out. He slowly approached the mound, and cautiously his hand reached for the cloth. For a moment, he stopped and withdrew his hand, but then his curiosity got the better of him. He pulled the piece of cloth that protruded from the mound. It seemed stuck. He pulled again and some snow fell off.

He trembled at the sight of a hand appearing. Oh no! Not here! He had seen movies on television where they find corpses in the snow, but that was fake. He did *not* want to find a real corpse! Not now, now that he was running away from those horrible people. He might have to go to the police, or worse they might think he did it!

All of a sudden his safe haven wasn't safe anymore. He had to move on.

He jumped back when a noise sounded from the snow heap. He stared wide-eyed at his find that rippled with the snow that fell off it. He took another step back when a small critter crawled out of the mound and gave a brief yelp. It sat there blinking in the bright daylight with its round black eyes. He looked at the small animal, then moved closer to pick it up. 'Hello there,' he said. The timid little animal crawled against the mound, evading his outstretched hand. 'Come on, I won't hurt you.' The animal let out another short yelp as if to warn him not to come closer.

The mound stirred, and he started away from it. A soft moan sounded, and the cloth moved. Maybe the corpse wasn't dead after all ! it went through his head. As the mound moved, more snow fell from it and soon arms, legs and a face came into view. The face looked like that of a corpse; it was so white. As white as the snow itself.

'Are you dead?' he asked.

The figure moved, and a hand reached for his. The lips in the face tried to form words: 'Help me'. Words that could barely be heard. He stood there, not eager to touch a dead hand, but when he looked into the face and saw the eyes, he reached out and tried pulling her up. The hand was freezing cold. Maybe she had frostbite. He once knew someone who had to have fingers amputated because of frostbite. She shivered and felt as cold as the snow itself. Maybe she was an Ice Queen! She looked like an Ice Queen with her short dark hair sticking out like frozen spikes. It looked like she was wearing a crown. Wouldn't that be something! Maybe she had come to help him, maybe that's why he was 'sent here'!

'Please ... ' she managed to say, 'please ... where's the warmth ... '

Her lips quivered as she said it.

'Better lean on me and I'll take you to my barn,' he said. The little animal that tried to patter after them almost drowned in the snow. '... M m my dog,' she shivered. 'P.. p please ... t take him.'

Her dog, he thought, he'd never seen such a small

critter of a dog.

When they reached the barn door, he released the young woman to clear the entrance of snow so she could go through. 'We need to make you a fire,' he said. 'We need to get some dry wood.'

He helped her into the barn and down onto the hay. 'I will look for some wood,' he said and started to walk outside. The young lady shook her head. 'Not … out there, is all wet f .. frozen.'

He didn't understand, where else to get wood out here than in the forest? He looked around and noticed some planks leaning against the barn wall.

'Those will have to do then,' he decided. He broke chunks off the planks and put them down in the middle of the barn on the muddy floor, away from the hay. He took some matches from his bag and with a handful of hay for kindling he set the pieces of wood on fire. Sputtering at first because of its dampness, but soon he had the fire going.

The young lady had observed him from where she was sitting. 'You've done this before, have you,' she quietly said.

He didn't answer. 'Come sit here, near the fire. You need to get warm.'

She looked at him and did what he had told her. He couldn't be more than ten years old, and yet, he seemed more mature somehow.

'What's your name?' she asked and sat down next to him by the fire.

He looked into the flames. 'You can call me Ben … And yours? What's your name?'

'Laura,' she said. 'Laura Everett-Jones.'

He looked at her. 'Why a double name? Are you married?

She shook her head. 'No. It's just how it is.'

'How did you end up here, on the road?' Ben asked.

Laura gave a start at that remark. 'Oh, my chauffeur!' she cried out. 'My chauffeur is still in the car!'

'Your chauffeur?' The lady had a *chauffeur* that brought her here?

'Oh Ben, we hit a tree and he was full of blood! I … I just went for help!' She fumbled through her pockets, but they were empty. 'I must have lost it,' she said, discouraged.

Ben looked at her with inquisitive eyes.

'My phone, I must've lost it in the snow,' Laura clarified.

Ben stood up when he noticed a can lying on the ground. He wiped it clean and put some snow in it. Then he placed it on the fire. 'What's that for?' Laura wanted to know.

'Tea. I wouldn't mind a nice cup-of-tea.'

Again, Ben impressed Laura who found the boy rather grown-up in his manner. 'Did you take any teabags then?'

He didn't answer but reached for his bag and took out a teabag. He put it in the can of water that began to boil on the fire.

'You must be with the Boy Scouts,' Laura said.

'Are you feeling warmer?' Ben asked.

'Much better, thank you.' She petted her little dog that lay nestled in her lap.

'What's his name?'

'It's a she, actually. Her name is Suzy.'

Suzy, what kind of name is that for a dog? Ben wondered, but the dog suited her. A silly lap dog for a person who was silly enough to go out driving with her *chauffeur* in that horrible weather.

'Maybe they have found your car by now,' Ben said.

'Maybe now, now that the weather has cleared up, you can just see it and when people pass they will check it out.' That thought worried him because if the car was found, it meant that they could be found too.

'I hope so,' Laura said. 'In any case, we can't stay here. We need to find a way back to civilisation.'

Ben looked into the flames that started to die. 'I'd better put some more wood on it.'

Laura watched him as he tended to the fire. 'How did you end up here?' she asked. 'Do you live around here?'

Ben didn't like lying, but he nodded. In a way, though, he wasn't lying. He was from 'around here'.

'Look, I need to go,' he abruptly decided. 'I'm sure you'll manage now.' He grabbed his bag and rushed out of the barn.

'Hey!' Laura yelled after him.

Ben ran, he didn't want to explain anything, and she would be fine. She and her dog. 'Silly little monster,' he mumbled. He ran onto the forest lane as he had done not long before. Then, elated with his newfound freedom, but all had become a threat. Why did she have to lie there? Why had he felt he had to help her? Had anybody ever helped *him*? No. He had to find his own way, and he knew that no one could be trusted. He thought the 'parents' at his last foster home were nice people, even though he sensed they couldn't be trusted, but at least he had a roof over his head and food on his plate every day. But that had not lasted long. Soon 'nice' Mrs Morton started to give him less and less food whenever her husband was away while stuffing her face with whatever she liked to cook for her and her child while he went to bed hungry.

When her husband, 'nice' Mr Morton, came home she complained that 'James wouldn't eat'. Something that always resulted in beatings for James' unappreciative behaviour. Ben fought back the tears. He kept running, the memory of the beatings made him run even faster, afraid that they might be right behind him and catch him. After the last beating, Ben had decided to leave that awful place. He had taken food from the pantry behind Mrs M's back; there was always so much there, she wouldn't notice. He even managed to take some money from her purse, packed his bag and left that house by climbing through his window at dead of night. The decision to change his name from James to Ben had been an easy one as he had once overheard that it was his real father's name.

Ben felt out of breath and plunged in the snow by the side of the forest path. He stuffed some snow into his mouth. 'I'm never going back to civilisation,' he muttered. 'I will stay here.'

The Ice Queen would be leaving the barn, she would look for her car and her chauffeur, and they would all leave. Then he would go back to his barn. He had to plan for his future. Ben stood up and looked in the direction of his barn. He could start walking back and keep a distance and make sure they were all gone. Then he would go back into his barn.

Laura tucked her little Chihuahua into her coat and climbed over the fence. She had no idea which way she had come the night before, nor any idea where she was but hoped that the field she was trying to walk through would lead her to a farmhouse of some kind. The night before, after another disagreement with her mother, she had decided to leave her parental home. Laura hadn't felt the need to understand why, in this day, her parents still kept to ancient notions of marrying 'one's own kind'. She was in love with Geoff, and it was him she wanted to marry. He was a good man, an artist and didn't have money, but money isn't everything. And after all, she had money. Her grandparents' money was put in a Trust for her. She didn't care what her mother and father thought about her relationship with Geoff. She wanted Geoff to spend Christmas with her and the family at Whittington Hall, but her mother refused. She didn't want a 'commoner' at her table at Christmas. A commoner! Her mother could be such a snob. Just because *she* was born into money didn't mean that other people were lesser beings. Laura stumbled through the snow-drifts in the field, which was covered in a thick layer of snow. She sank knee-deep into the icy white fluff. Her legs felt cold, she wasn't wearing proper shoes for this kind of weather. She never thought she would have to walk through such thick snow, the morning after rushing out of the house with only one bag, and Suzy snuggled up inside her warm winter coat. Mark had been the only available chauffeur, and he had agreed to drive her. She hadn't really known where she wanted to go, just somewhere where she wouldn't have to deal with her parents for a few days. The blizzard had come so unexpectedly. She felt hungry. The hot tea the boy had prepared had been a welcome gift; it even contained sugar. Where had he gone? He shot out of that barn, like an arrow from a bow. And why would he carry teabags and sugar in his bag? Maybe he was on one of those Boy Scouts survival trips. She hoped he would go and get help. Laura looked behind her, holding a cupped hand against her forehead to shield her eyes from the sun's glare, its brightness was reflecting in the white of the snow. The barn in the distance was now just a speck, surrounded by the skeletons of the trees. She must seem an even smaller speck in the immense desert of snow. There were no footprints other than the ones she had left. In front of her, on the other side of the glistening white blanket, she noticed another structure at the edge of the field. Could it be a farmhouse? The sight of it made her walk faster as best she could. 'Here we go, Suzy.' The tiny critter with her little black dot of a nose smelled the air as if to determine if the warm nest was nearby. Bravely, Laura tramped through the field, the house was getting closer with every step. She stopped when she thought she saw motion near the house and noticed a car hidden half behind it. She let out a relieved sigh. At least someone would be there. As she moved closer to the farmhouse, she began to doubt whether her eyes had not deceived her. The house looked quite deserted. When she reached the fence that parted the yard from the field a shock went through her body. She saw the car she escaped from during the fierce storm in the night by the road in front of the house. How did that get there? She saw one side completely dented and the back door half-open. At the same time, she felt joy, for if the car was there, Mark should be all right. He must have recovered and sought help! Laura rushed to the house. The windows looked like mirrors with the sun shining straight at them. She pressed her face against a window and looked through. There wasn't anyone in the room as far as she could see. The noise of a slamming door made her look up.

'Don't let him out of your sight ... ' a voice said, followed by footsteps on the frozen path. Laura peeked around the corner of the house and saw a man walking to the parked car. Suzy made a snarling noise inside Laura's coat, who instantly knew what that meant. Laura swiftly moved back and pressed against the wall until she heard the car pull away. Carefully, she took a look and saw the car follow the road. Where the strong winds had kept it free of snow, the car could easily continue at a speed that was not allowed on these narrow roads. She walked around the house and glanced through a window at the back. A man was standing by a table, an unfamiliar man.

'Oh my god!' she uttered. There, sitting half-turned was Mark. Her chauffeur! Good man! He had found a rescuer. She felt an urge to rush into the house and thank him, and then they could all go home when the stranger slapped Mark across his face. He fell to the floor, chair and all. 'What the … ' Laura started. She now noticed Mark's hands tied around the back of the chair on which he was sitting. 'Oh my god,' she expressed once more. Laura quickly left the window and rushed back to where she initially stood. She held her breath at the sound of fast approaching footsteps and before she could do anything the strange man cast his shadow over her and grabbed her roughly by her arm. 'What have we here?' His voice sounded angry and threatening at the same time. While Suzy snarled under her coat, the man dragged her with him; Laura could barely stay on her feet. He pushed her into the house where Mark was still lying on the floor with the chair tied to him. The man threw Laura in a corner. Suzy fell from her warm hideaway and onto the floor as well.

'Friend of yours?' he demanded. Mark looked at Laura with beckoning eyes. Laura crawled in his direction. 'Mark, are you all right? Were you badly hurt?' She sat next to him and looked at his face that was black and blue on one side and still covered in dried blood. 'Oh Mark,' she said compassionately.

'Is this the girl?!' the stranger ordered. He walked over to Laura and grabbed her arm. 'What's your name!'

Laura felt anger boiling up inside of her and as she got to her feet she tore herself free from the grip the man had on her. 'None of your business,' she hissed through her teeth. The blow the man then gave her, made her lose her balance and fall onto the floor again.

There were certain things people should *never* do to Laura Everett-Jones, and hitting her was one of them. From the corner of her eye, Laura saw the man walk back to Mark. She got to her feet and grabbed one of the chairs that were by the table. With all her strength, she started to beat the man on his head with it. Hit him until he, too, was lying on the floor with blood streaming from his head. She looked at him with fiery eyes. 'Don't you *ever* lay your filthy hands on me again,' she hissed in his face.

'Laura … ' Mark's voice sounded. Laura went towards him while keeping a constant eye on the stranger. 'Laura, we need to leave this place quickly, the other one might come back soon.'

'I know,' Laura said matter-of-factly. She started undoing the rope that kept Mark tied to the chair, and soon he was on his feet. 'The car isn't working,' he said. Laura tied the stranger's feet and hands with the rope previously used for Mark.

'How did it get here then?' she asked. With the danger briefly out of the way, poor Suzy came over to Laura and crawled onto her lap. 'I'll explain later,' Mark said. He felt his head. 'Let's go.'

Laura gave the stranger one more look before following her chauffeur out of the house, tucking little Suzy into her coat. 'How did you get here then?' she asked again.

Mark stumbled ahead, holding his hand against his head. 'It hurts like hell,' he muttered. 'They found me, in the car. As you know, that isn't your average Mini … '

'Christ,' Laura uttered. 'Bastards.'

'They dragged me into their car and tied the Jag behind it. That's how we got here.'

'Don't people have any decency anymore?' Laura

said. 'Kidnapping a wounded man!'

'I heard them say something like, they could do it up and sell it,' Mark explained 'They … they hadn't really decided what they were going to do with me … '

Laura walked around the Jaguar that wasn't of any use to them in its present state. 'The keys are still in it,' she said. She opened the door at the passenger's seat and took them. 'I won't give them the pleasure.'

'Laura, those petty thieves will find ways to get it going. Now let's go!' He had seen a car in the distance fast approaching.

'Wait,' Laura said. 'My bag. It has muesli bars in it. I'm starving.' She crawled through the half-open back door and reached under the front seat.

'Laura, hurry up! It's him.'

Mark grabbed Laura's arm. 'Quick! In that ditch!'

Mark looked up to see the car coming before he, too, jumped into the ditch by the road. Poor Suzy yelped a painful cry. 'Oh sorry, Suze,' Laura said. 'God you're so tiny, sometimes I don't even feel you're there.'

Mark pushed her head down. 'Quiet,' he whispered.

Bent down, they waited until the noise of the car had stopped, after it had turned onto the yard by the house. Mark looked at Laura, who knew their escape would soon be known. She peeked over the snowy drift and saw the driver of the car enter the house.

'Oh no,' Mark uttered, startled. Before he could stop her, Laura ran across the road and opened the car door. As she jumped in, Mark saw movement inside the house. 'Oh no,' he said again, but when the car backed up, turned around and sped in his direction, he jumped out of the ditch and into the car.

'Haahaaa,' Laura laughed as she looked in the rearview mirror and saw one of the man trying to catch the car and its occupants. It was a pathetic attempt. Laura watched him become smaller by the second until he appeared as a mere black dot on the road that was surrounded by the white snow. 'That'll teach them!' Laura happily called out. She looked beside her, towards Mark, only to see that his head had fallen onto his chest and his eyes were closed. 'Mark! Mark!'

She drove the car around a bend in the road and stopped. She took his head in her hands. 'Mark!' There was no reaction. 'Oh God, no.' She looked at his face when slowly one of his eyes opened. 'Mark, are you all right?'

Mark let out a deep sigh. 'I ... passed out ... my head hurts like hell ... ' he uttered.

'OK, no time to lose,' Laura decided. 'Hospital.'

She drove the car back onto the road and sped off, not really knowing where she was going.

'Mark, do you know where we are?'

Mark slowly moved his head. ' ... Last night, before that blizzard hit, we were heading up the  motorway ... Until you decided you wanted the scenic route ... '

'Where was that then?'

Mark opened the car window and let the cold wind blow across his face. 'Uhm, I think,' he said, wiping his face with his hand, 'somewhere near Junction 7, I think, if I remember correctly.'

'Junction 7. That's near ... Where is that near? Manchester?'

'Accrington,' Mark affirmed. Laura sighed. 'We need to get to Manchester if we are to deliver you at a *proper* hospital.'

The skeletal trees and green pines that broke the white of the snow around them became fewer in number the farther they drove. A secondary road emerged from the forest road until the motorway came into view, but just before they reached a junction, the car started to miss. Laura looked at the petrol meter. 'It still has enough,' she said.

Mark tapped it. 'It's broke,' he determined as the car let out its last splutter. Laura looked discontented. 'Great.' There they were with civilisation in view and a car that had no intention of taking them there. 'Well, better eat something first. I can think better when I have eaten,' she said as she pulled her bag from under the seat. She handed Mark one of the muesli bars and took one herself. 'You must be starving too. Did they give you *any*thing?'

' ... No.'

Laura looked in her rearview mirror when she noticed movement and the brief sound of a siren. Then glanced over her shoulder to see if the reflection in the mirror had been correct. 'Mark! It's the police!'

She was about to get out of the car, but a policeman had already reached them and tapped on the window. 'Miss, will you pl ... '

'Oh, *so* glad you're here,' Laura interrupted him. 'Please, get us to a hospital.'

'Miss, your driving licence, please,' the officer said.

'Please,' Laura begged. 'Can't you see? Mark needs a doctor.'

The police officer motioned his colleague, who had remained in the patrol car, to come.

'Miss, your driving licence, please.' This time the policeman sounded more resolute.

Laura looked at Mark. 'I don't have one,' she then quietly stated. 'My father's chauffeurs always drive me.'

'Oh, really?' the police officer said. 'Would you please step out of the car?'

Laura took her bag and made sure Suzy was safely

inside her coat before she stepped out of the car.

'Did your *father's chauffeurs* never tell you that it is forbidden to drive stolen cars?'

The other policeman had reached them and was by the passenger's side.

'Can't you see he needs help?' Laura pleaded. 'I don't care what you do with me, but please, take Mark to a hospital.'

The police officers looked at each other. 'We'll get him to a hospital. But did you know you're driving a stolen car?'

'Yes!' Laura called out. 'We took it from those petty thieves who kidnapped Mark! Now please, we'll explain on the way.' She walked towards the police car, quickly followed by the police officer.

'Mark! Come, *they* are taking us.'

The other policeman made sure Mark didn't go anywhere but in the police car. Laura sat down in the back, and one of the policemen sat down beside her. Mark was pushed onto the back seat as well.

'You will *have* to believe me,' Laura said. 'We were caught in that snowstorm last night and the car hit a tree, and then I went for help and fell in the snow and then this boy came and saved me and then I went to this house and saw these men had tied Mark up and then we escaped and took their car and … '

'All right, all right,' the police officer said. 'We'll take your friend here to the hospital, and we'll take *you* in.'

'Good!' Laura expressed.


Lord Everett-Jones emerged from his limousine and looked up at the façade of the police station. The expression on his face wasn't one of amusement. He energetically took the few steps to the entrance of the building and walked through its brown doors and entered the hall. He looked around and walked towards the reception area. 'I'm here to see my daughter,' he said.

'Your name, Sir?'

'Everett-Jones.'

The receptionist briefly glanced up at his face. 'I'll tell them you're here, Sir,' she said as she took the telephone off the receiver. Lord Everett-Jones turned and had another look around the building he so unexpectedly had to come to. His demeanour showed impatience and at the same time self-confidence. It was clear he was not someone to be tangled with.

'You can go through,' the receptionist said. By way of thanks, Lord Everett-Jones gave her a brief nod, then walked swiftly to the door she had indicated; his long coat gracefully tailing behind him as walked. When he opened the door, he entered into an office where he saw a few police officers seated behind their desks. He was just about to inquire when he noticed his daughter sitting on a bench against the wall. Laura looked at the man who had just entered until he spread out his arms. Laura jumped up to receive her father's embrace. 'Really, Daddy, we haven't done anything wrong,' her muffled voice sounded in his waistcoat. 'It was a horrid night!'

One of the police officers stood up and walked towards them. 'You're the father?'

'Yes,' Lord Everett-Jones declared.

'Your daughter placed herself in a rather unpleasant situation. Found driving a car without a licence … '

'I had to!' Laura rebuked. 'Mark was hurt … ' Her father motioned her to keep quiet.

' … driving a stolen car,' the police officer continued, 'and we've just had a report in, stating that stolen goods were found in the boot of that stolen car, along with 50 grams of cocaine.'

'What!' Laura uttered.

'I must ask you, Sir, but has your daughter ever been involved in drugs?'

'No,' Lord Everett-Jones resolutely stated. 'Never. Absolutely not.'

'We also checked her story about the house where *petty thieves* held her friend Mark captive … '

'He's not a friend as such,' Lord Everett-Jones said, 'he's on my pay-roll. He's a chauffeur.'

'Very well, but there was no sign of anything in that house she indicated.'

Laura looked at the police officer with disbelieve. 'Are you sure you checked the right house? They also took the Jaguar, Daddy. It had a huge dent on the side but Mark said they would repair it and sell the car for lots of money.'

The police officer glanced at Laura. 'I think your daughter has a wild imagination, Sir … '

Lord Everett-Jones' grey eyes turned cold as he looked at him. 'My daughter does not lie, officer. Are you sure you and your men have done their job duly?'

'Look, there was no Jaguar and there was no blood on the floor. And no Boy Scouts on survival trips,' the police officer defended the case, resting his gaze on Laura.

'Right then,' Lord Everett-Jones decided. 'Laura, you come with me and show me where all this happened. But first, give your mother a call. She's demented with worry.'

With a sigh, the police officer indicated that Laura could use the phone on his desk. 'You will have to stand bail, Sir,' he then addressed Mr Everett-Jones who, without hesitation, took out a cheque-book. 'How much?'

Lord Everett-Jones put an arm around his daughter's shoulder as they walked to the limousine. 'Was the Jaguar badly damaged?' he asked. 'You know how fond I am of that car.'

Laura looked up at her father's face. 'Daddy … '

'Well, you have your favourites, don't you?' He opened the back door of the limousine. 'Let's see if we can find it,' he said. 'That, and the rest the police have failed to produce.'

He sat next to his daughter in the back seat. Laura put little Suzy in between them and told her father's driver where he needed to take them. The car was set in motion and smoothly pulled out of the street; on its sides, the snow was swept up in low heaps. They drove out of the city and onto the motorway. Only yesterday, Laura had wanted to go there in an attempt to avoid her parents. At junction seven along the same road, they turned off and continued until the secondary road eventually became the forest road. The scenery seemed somewhat unfamiliar, bathed in the shadows of the late afternoon, but Laura was positive they were heading in the right direction. She saw the scenery coming their way, conversant with what she had seen in the rearview mirror of the car she and Mark had used to get away in. Laura looked out the car window and saw the field she had walked through only that morning. 'There,' she said. 'There's the farmhouse.'

Her father's chauffeur, Donald Mullins, slowed down and stopped by the side of the road. Laura viewed the surroundings that showed no signs of people being around. 'The Jaguar was right there,' she expressed.

'Well, let's go and see,' her father said and took the door handle to get out of the car. Laura followed his example. She slowly walked towards the spot where her father's favourite but damaged car had been parked. There were only tracks, clearly visible in the snow. Laura pointed to them. 'I can't believe the police missed those,' she said.

'They're clear enough,' Lord Everett-Jones conceded. 'Let's check the house.' He glanced over to Mullins, who had emerged from the car and stood leant against the door by the driver's seat.

'Keep an eye on Suzy, will you Donald?' Laura requested as she took the narrow path that led to the back door; the door she was so roughly dragged through by one of the men earlier in the day. Her father, right in front of her, grabbed the door handle and opened the door. 'Mm,' he uttered. 'Not even locked.'

They stepped into the house and entered the kitchen that Laura recognised as the room where Mark was beaten and tied to the chair, which was still half under the table on its side. Laura quickly walked towards the spot. 'Look, Daddy,' she pointed, 'there is still blood. Look!'

Lord Everett-Jones came nearer and bent down to see. 'You're right,' he concluded. 'Well, Laura, it appears the police are either blind or have investigated the wrong house.' He straightened his back and had another look around the basic kitchen. 'So, here's where those criminals were hiding.'

He walked towards a door that faced the entrance and opened it. Behind it was a staircase. He looked up and then closed the door again. 'I'm sure they fled, taking the Jaguar with them. We'd better go, inform the police.'

Laura followed her father as he walked out of the kitchen when she heard a shuffling sound above her. 'Daddy,' she whispered.

'What?'

'I heard something.' She pointed to the ceiling.

'Are you sure?' her father asked. Laura nodded.

'Probably mice,' her father said and opened the kitchen door when they heard a thump.

Slowly Lord Everett-Jones closed the door and quietly walked back into the house with Laura holding on to his coat sleeve. 'Mice don't make that much noise,' he said in a quiet voice. 'Maybe a cat,' Laura whispered.

Mr Everett-Jones walked back to the door he had opened only moments earlier. This time he walked up the narrow staircase, vigilantly. Laura followed his movements closely when she heard the door opened behind her. Fright appeared in her face, and she slowly moved her head in the direction of the sound. Then, she let out a relieved sigh.

'Donald,' she said. 'Please … '

'Sorry, Miss,' Donald said, 'but I saw movement on the first floor. Where's … ?'

Suddenly, like an arrow from a bow, a boy flew passed them. 'Grab him!' they heard calling from above followed by the thundering footsteps of Lord Everett-Jones.

Donald jumped towards the boy and grabbed him by the shoulder. 'Stop! You little devil!' he exclaimed.

Laura was pleasantly surprised. She walked towards Donald, who had a firm grip on the struggling boy. 'Ben,' Laura said. 'Oh Ben, I'm so glad it's you.' She took Ben's arm. 'No need to be afraid.'

The boy looked at her with an angry face. 'Why did you bring them here! I *knew* you couldn't be trusted!'

'Please, Ben. Don't be angry, it's just my father … ' With apprehension, Ben looked up at the man who still had his hand upon his shoulder. 'No, not him,' Laura explained. 'He's my daddy's chauffeur.'

'Oh, for heaven's sake, Ice Queen, how many *chauffeurs* do you have? I think you have the police after

me! That's what I think!' Ben pulled himself free from
Donald Mullins' grip. Lord Everett-Jones came closer and
looked at the boy. 'And why would you think that, boy?'

Ben retreated from the people who so uninvited had
interrupted his way to freedom. Laura came towards him
and put her hands on his shoulders. 'Ben, I told you,
there's nothing to be afraid of. We're just here to see what
has happened to Daddy's Jaguar and catch those
criminals.'

Ben glanced up at Laura. 'They've gone,' he softly
said. 'I saw them. They fixed something and then drove
off with that car. Even though it had a huge dent in it.'
Ben emphasized the word huge. 'I heard them say, they
said they were going to Liverpool.'

Laura hugged Ben. 'You're sweet, you know that?'

Ben gave her a puzzling look.

'Liverpool?' Lord Everett-Jones wondered. 'Well.
Mullins, we'd better go back to the police station and
explain to them what we know.'

Ben ripped himself free from Laura's embrace. 'Uh,
I'm sorry, Sir, but I have to go now.'

'That's fine, we're all going,' Lord Everett-Jones said.
'Tell Mullins where you need to be and we'll drop you
off.'

'Beg your pardon, Sir,' Donald said, 'but the police
might want a statement from the boy. He'd better come
with us first.'

'Good point … ' and with those last words from
Laura's father, Ben shot out of the kitchen and ran into the
yard. 'Ben!' Laura called after him. 'Ben! Come back!'

She ran out of the house too, closely followed by her
father and Donald. Ben ran around the house and into the
fields where Laura followed him. She felt pleased that no
new snow had fallen during the day, for the walk through

the same field that morning had been difficult enough.

'After them,' Lord Everett-Jones ordered and he and Mullins also made their way into the field that already emitted the greyness of the oncoming evening. Laura struggled to reach Ben, who, even though he was two heads shorter than Laura, still managed to stay ahead of her. Ben ran as fast as his legs could carry him through the snow, but Laura, with her long, slender legs had the advantage. She soon gained and the distance between her and Ben diminished. 'Ben! Please!' she called out when she was finally able to grab him by his shoulder and stop him from running any further. 'What's with you? Why are you running away?'

Ben turned to her, panting. This time, his determination seemed to have left him. 'Please,' he begged, 'please, let me go. I don't want to go with you! I don't want to go to any police station!'

'But, why on earth not?' Laura expressed. 'All you need to do is tell them what you've overheard and then we'll take you home.'

Ben looked past Laura and saw Lord Everett-Jones and Mullins gaining ground. 'Because ... because ... '

'Yes?' Laura asked. Ben cast his gaze downwards. 'I don't have a home,' he then said. When he looked up at Laura, she saw a tear rolling down his cheek. 'Oh, Ben. It can't be that bad. Everybody has a home to go to,' she said with empathy.

'No!' Ben shouted in her face. 'Not everybody has a home to go to! You, you and all your chauffeurs and your father and ... ' Ben couldn't help it, but the tension of the last few days finally got the better of him and tears started to flow down his cheeks. 'I only have those horrible people!'

'Oh, Ben.' She tried to calm him down. 'You

shouldn't say that about your parents ...'

'They're not my parents!'

Gasping for breath, Lord Everett-Jones and Mullins had reached them and looked at the crying boy. 'Laura,' her father said, 'what *have* you done to him?'

'Please, Daddy. I think we'd better go now.' She put an arm around Ben's shoulder and took him back with them. 'You'd better explain your situation when we're in the car,' she said to him. 'It's no fun being out here at night in the freezing cold and darkness.'

The evening had descended on the city, and Lord Everett-Jones, Laura and Mullins found themselves sitting on a bench in the police station. A certain officer had just been told where the police should gather evidence for further investigation.

'Did he call you *Ice Queen*?' Lord Everett-Jones asked his daughter.

'What, Daddy?'

'Ben. He called you Ice Queen.'

'Yes, he did, didn't he,' Laura conceded. 'I haven't told you about my ordeal, but it was Ben who found me early this morning. After Mark and I crashed into that tree and Mark appeared to be in a bad condition, I wanted to get help.'

Her father looked surprised. 'Why didn't you just use your phone?'

'No network. We were out there and there was no network. So, I got out of the car and started walking ... '

'Oh dear. Laura Everett-Jones, sometimes you can be *very* irresponsible.'

'Yes, well. I don't know how long I walked and I started to feel cold. The only thing that kept me warm was Suzy's little body in my coat. Dear Suzy,' she said, petting her tiny Chihuahua that lay peacefully in her lap. 'I must have fallen at some point, and next thing I knew Suzy yelped, and it was daylight. That's when Ben found me … I must have looked like an Ice Queen with my hair in frozen locks on top of my head.'

Lord Everett-Jones looked at his daughter in horror. 'Laura, darling! You could have frozen to death!' he exclaimed. 'You will *not* go out on your own again. I *won't* allow it!'

'I'm sorry, Daddy.'

'Thank *God*, the boy was there. Thank God he found you.'

'Dear Ben, he's a sweet boy. He made me hot tea in that barn. I think that's where he'd set up camp … '

'Set up camp indeed.'

'Well at least it was warm there and then … Then he just left, just like he did when we were at the farmhouse.' She looked in the direction of the door that had just opened. Ben walked in, followed by a police officer. 'Can I have a word with you, Sir?' the latter addressed Lord Everett-Jones.

'Certainly,' was the answer. Lord Everett-Jones stood up, leaving space for Ben to sit down. He followed the police officer into his office and sat in the chair the policeman had indicated. 'Well, that was quite a story the boy told me,' the officer said as he, too, sat down. Lord Everett-Jones, not really a man for social mumbo-jumbo, looked at him. 'Yes, well. Better tell me then.'

'He ran away from a foster home. Uh … we have contacted the responsible authority. He ran away from the people that were caring for him.'

'Why?'

'He says he was beaten. On a regular basis.'

'No wonder.'

'What, Sir?'

'No wonder, he ran away.'

'Well, we still need to investigate that of course. Children tell so many … uh … stories.'

Lord Everett-Jones wasn't satisfied with that answer.

'Did you have the poor boy examined by a doctor? Does Ben have, let's say, traces? Of beatings?'

The police officer shook his head. 'Not yet, Sir.'

Lord Everett-Jones looked at the policeman. 'Is that another issue you allow the general public to investigate?'

The police officer showed slight embarrassment. 'No Sir. We have just called a GP. And another thing, the boy's name is James, not Ben.'

'Ben, James. Does it matter? When will the doctor be here?'

'The boy needs to go *there*, Sir. Then the doctor sends us the report.'

Lord Everett-Jones sighed for the tiresome policing ways. 'I've a better idea, officer. The boy is coming home with us and I will have him examined by our family doctor. He will send you his findings. How does that sound?'

The police officer seemed indecisive.

'Look here, officer, I won't have the boy placed in some Home. That boy practically saved my daughter's life today! He's coming home with us.'

'If you insist, Sir. That's very kind of you. You will be notified when Child Welfare have found him a new home.'

Lord Everett-Jones stood up, 'Yes, well, we'll see about that,' he said, shaking the policeman's hand. 'You know where to contact me.'

He walked out of the office to find the others waiting patiently for him, with Ben having allowed little Suzy onto his lap and showing an increased liking to the small creature.

'Time to go home,' Lord Everett-Jones told them. 'Mullins, please drive the car in front.'

More snow had fallen during the night, but the morning was clear, all though grey clouds were approaching in the distance. Ben had climbed onto a chair and looked out of one of the windows of the room where he slept. The sky was beautiful, and the sun shone its icy glow on the park surrounding the enormous house. Ben felt like going out and running around in the snow and building a snowman! He had always wanted to make a snowman, but whenever there had been a little snow, he had never been allowed out long enough. He could barely take his eyes off the wide landscape around the house. So much snow! He could make a million snowmen! But, maybe it wasn't allowed. He probably should ask, but what if they said no? He lowered himself from the chair and strolled around the large room. A room so big he could easily share it with his friends from the Children's Home where he lived when he was not placed with a foster family.

He knew that he couldn't stay here. Laura's parents were very kind, but Ben knew his stay here was only a temporary solution. He would have to leave as soon as Child Welfare found him another foster home. He could only hope that it would be with nice people.

Laura's mother had said that the Mortons had been arrested. That news had pleased him. Served them right, let them sit in jail! Laura's mother had been outraged: '*Five* days dear Ben was gone and they hadn't even reported him missing! Have you ever heard of such a thing! Fraudulent monsters!' That's what she had called them, monsters. And she was right. Laura's mother had said also that these people had 'cheated the system' and that's why the police had come to arrest them.

His door flew open, and Laura entered. 'Good morning, Ben. How are you today?'

Ben shrugged. 'Fine,' he said. Laura had been very kind to him, too, the days he'd been here, but sometimes she was so … girlish towards him and he wasn't sure if he liked all that affection; especially as he had to leave again.

'Breakfast is waiting,' Laura said, cheerfully.

Ben walked to the door. 'Let's go then,' he said.

'I went to see Mark yesterday,' Laura continued. 'Poor man, he has a broken cheekbone and a slight concussion.' Ben glanced up at her face. 'Is he one of your chauffeurs?'

'Yes. Well, he works for Daddy.'

They walked up the landing and down the broad staircase that led to the hallway that led to the dining-room, or at least to one of the rooms where they were used to having their meals. Ben found it all a bit over the top. How many rooms does a house need anyway? This house was more like a hotel. They entered the breakfast room, where Suzy lay curled up in her basket in the corner.

'Morning, Ben,' Lady Everett-Jones said as the two entered. 'Darling,' she addressed her daughter.

'Morning, Mummy,' Laura replied. Less cheerful than a few moments earlier, Ben observed. He took a plate from the side-board and filled it with toast and eggs before sitting down at the table. The food was very nice here, he found.

'Slept well, Ben?' Lady Everett-Jones asked. Ben nodded.

'We will decorate the Christmas tree today. How does that sound, Ben?'

Ben's eyes lit up. 'Can I watch?'

'Of *course*,' Mrs Everett-Jones replied.

Laura looked at her mother and launched the subject once more. 'Mummy, I will invite Geoff to Christmas dinner whether you like it or not.'

Lady Everett-Jones glanced at her daughter. 'Laura darling, you know how Daddy and I feel about it. Why do you persist so?'

'Mummy, I love him. I want him with me at Christmas.'

'Fiddlesticks. What do you know about love? Darling, you're only nineteen, you haven't lived!'

'Oh, Mummy. How old were you when you met Daddy? No, let me tell you. You were eighteen! Now there!'

Ben looked on in wonder. He hoped they weren't going to fly at each other.

'Yes! Exactly, we *met* at eighteen, but we weren't married until we were twenty-three!'

Her mother had a complacent look on her face. 'Now there!'

Laura sighed. 'All right. But who says I want to get married now … '

'You did, darling! You said you wanted to marry that … Gerard, or whatever he's called.'

Laura looked displeased. 'His name is Geoff, Mother.'

Mrs Everett-Jones face softened. 'Either way, but how can you be so certain that he's *the one*?'

Laura's face clouded over. 'You were certain, Mother.'

'Yes, well. But I gave it five years!' she said and glanced over to Ben. 'Besides, your little brother needs you now. How would he feel if his family already abandons him?

Laura looked at her mother in disbelief. 'Mummy …
are you serious? A .. are you adopting Ben?'

Lady Everett-Jones showed a friendly smile. 'It's the
best your father and I could think of.'

Ben looked at Laura and then to Lady Everett-Jones;
Gerry to friends, she had said. He didn't know if they
were joking. Grown-ups can be strange sometimes, and
not to be trusted.

'So, is it official?' Laura requested of her mother.

'Of course, darling! Just some paperwork needs to be
sorted, but as far as we are concerned,' and she reached
for Ben's hand, 'Ben is part of our family from now on.'

Laura jumped up from her chair and ran to hug Ben.
'Ben! You're my little brother!'

'We couldn't possibly send him back to those horrid
Homes,' Lady Everett-Jones continued. 'We have so
much space, and Ben will have a good education.'

Ben showed joy but was ambivalent at the same time
when he looked in Lady Everett-Jones direction. 'Does
that mean … does that mean, you're my mother now?'

Mrs Everett-Jones gave him the sweetest smile he'd
seen in years. 'It means exactly that, my dear Ben.'

Laura ran from Ben to her mother whom she
showered with kisses.

'Don't overdo it, darling,' her mother said. 'Save
some for your boyfriend.'

Around Lady and Lord Everett-Jones' residence snow
had piled up. Ben and Laura's hard days' work were in
plain view, for two large snowmen stood on either side of
the stone steps leading up to the front door, welcoming
everyone who came to visit the family. Ben slowly walked
down one of the hallways of the large house; he still
wasn't quite used to its size. He stopped in front of one of

the high windows and looked at the fading daylight outside. The sky had changed colour to a darker blue and stars began to appear. He noticed the crescent moon dangling over some trees in the park. He'd learned it wasn't a park at all. They called it 'the garden'. He'd never seen such an enormous garden! Everything was so enormous here! He thought of his friends in the Children's Home. He wondered if their Christmas would be as good as his Christmas would be. He was sure that they would have good meals over the Holidays. At Christmas, the food at the Home was always good. The Mortons would have to spend their Christmas in prison. He couldn't help but feel relieved about that, and their son, that stuck-up prick, he'd be without his parents. Served him right. He thought of the man Ben, who they said was his real father. He never knew him, and he never met him. Maybe, he never even existed, but if he did exist, Ben was sure that he would be very happy that his son was living with a very nice family in a very nice home. Ben heard a shuffling sound and turned his head to see Lord Everett-Jones approach in the hall. He was a tall man and handsome too.

'Ben, there you are!' Lord Everett-Jones stood next to him and looked out the window as well. 'Beautiful evening,' he said. 'You and I should go out riding tomorrow. I'll show you the grounds.'

'Riding, Sir?'

'Horseback riding.'

'Sir, I don't know how to ride a horse, I … '

'You don't? Well, then you must learn. These grounds are wide spread, you can't possibly walk all that way.'

Ben smiled and looked up at Lord Everett-Jones.

'Thank you, Mr Everett-Jones.'

Lord Everett-Jones cleared his throat. 'Ben, do you

think … we could be a little less formal? You're practically our son.'

'OK, Sir … Dad,' Ben said and smiled at the thought. He had a father now!

'That's better … Oh, I think I can hear the guests arriving,' said Mr Everett-Jones and put an arm around Ben's shoulders. 'Let's meet them, shall we?'

Ben nodded as he tried to keep up with his father's stride.

'This will be a good Christmas,' the latter said. 'A very good Christmas.'

Ben agreed, wholeheartedly. 'The best Christmas ever.'

~.~

### *Vlokken*

Grote vlokken
kleine vlokken
veel vlokken
weinig vlokken
Vaag en traag, de zon
overspoeld door grijsheid
Meer vlokken
grote, kleine
Massa's wit

~.~

If you enjoyed reading this book, a review would be much appreciated for it will help others to discover these stories. Thank you!

Also by Caroline Muntjewerf:

Return To Les Jonquières

Bel Amour

Of Dutch Descent


Dutch:

Avondstond

*van* Hollandse Afkomst


German:

Holländische Wurzeln


~.~.~


https://cmuntjewerf.com

Printed in Great Britain
by Amazon